"Love In Silence

By

Tebogo Mathebula"

Love in Silence

A Romantic Memoir

© 2025 Tebogo Mathebula

or transmitted in any form or by any means, electronic, mechanical,

photocopying, recording, or otherwise, without prior written permission

of the author.

ISBN: 978-1-83492-476-2

Printed in South Africa

About the Author

Tebogo Mathebula is a storyteller of emotion, moments, and memory. Through poetic language and reflective narratives, he captures the gentle chaos of love, healing, and human connection. His writing explores the depths of relationships, the subtleties of human emotion, and the enduring power of love that transcends words and time.

With the Love in Silence series, Tebogo invites readers into intimate journeys of vulnerability, growth, and devotion, creating stories that resonate long after the final page is turned.

Preface

Love is often loud in stories, sung in grand gestures and spoken in declarations. Yet, some of the deepest connections are built in the quiet the glances, the unspoken understanding, the gentle presence beside you when words fail.

Love in Silence is my attempt to capture those moments. It is a reflection of my heart, my journey, and the lessons I've learned about love, vulnerability, and the courage it takes to let someone see your true self. Through these pages, you will meet Sunflower, a soul who challenged me, inspired me, and changed me in ways I never imagined.

This book is not just a story it is a space to feel, to reflect, and perhaps to recognize pieces of your own journey within mine. It is for the lovers who speak in whispers, the hearts that hold on, and the souls brave enough to embrace love even when it hurts.

As you read, may you find not just a story, but a mirror of your own silent moments, your own quiet triumphs, and the love that exists in the spaces between words.

Tebogo Mathebula

Table of Content

Chapter 1- *Love in Silence*

When the Quiet Spoke of You,before you ever said a word I felt you.

Your silence entered the room before your voice did and it was loud in ways only hearts can hear.
You sat near me, eyes scanning the world like it whispered secrets just for you. I wanted to ask what you were hearing, but instead I watched in awe. The quiet between us was never empty it was filled with things we were both too afraid to say.

You spoke with glances, with how your fingers curled around your cup, how your feet tapped gently when lost in thought. You were stillness wrapped in stories I hadn't yet read.

And in that stillness, I found myself listening more not to what you said, but to how you existed.

Sometimes, silence holds more truth than words ever could.
And your silence?
It taught me how to feel.

Always listening,
Muse

Midnight Drives & Echoes of Her,I
remember the night drive. The city lights
blurred as we drove past our favorite spots
not saying much, but saying everything.

You looked out the window, your reflection
pressed against the glass like a memory
already forming. I stole glances not because I
was unsure, but because looking at you felt
like witnessing something sacred.

I remember the way your hum filled the car,
how the wind played with your hair, how even
the quiet songs sounded louder with you next
to me.

I didn't want to arrive. I didn't want the drive
to end. Because something about you in that
stillness, in the midnight air felt like peace I
hadn't known in years.

Even now, when the road is empty and the
music plays low, I still hear echoes of you
humming softly, like the night is trying to
bring you back to me.

Still driving in memory,
Muse.

The Softness Behind Her Eyes, there was a softness in your gaze that undid me not because it was gentle, but because it saw straight through the armor I wore so well.

You looked at me like I wasn't broken. Like I was just in the middle of becoming.

You never rushed me to explain myself. You never forced healing. You just sat with me, asked questions with your eyes, and waited for me to come forward when I was ready.

I never told you, but in every glance, you reminded me that softness isn't weakness it's courage wrapped in warmth.

And I was terrified of it. Because I had spent so long building walls, I forgot what it felt like to be seen without them.

Thank you for seeing the version of me I was too afraid to believe in.

Always soft when I think of you,
Muse.

Moments That Linger Like, some memories don't just visit they linger. Like a scent that clings to your clothes long after the person has gone.

Your perfume still shows up in places you've never been. In elevators. On strangers. In bookstores. And every time, it stops me in my tracks.

I remember that day in the rain your laugh echoing as we ran under one small umbrella. I remember the warmth of your fingers in mine. The way you'd trace my palm like you were reading a map to something sacred.

There are songs I can't listen to without seeing your smile. Foods I can't taste without thinking of your joy. Days I can't live without stumbling into one more moment where you once were.

Some people leave. Others linger.
You, Sunflower you linger.

Still carrying the scent,
Muse.

The First Goodbye That Wasn't Said,not all goodbyes come with warnings.
Some arrive slowly in silence, in distance, in the way we stop finishing each other's sentences.

I didn't know we were saying goodbye when you stopped replying as often. When your eyes stopped lighting up when I walked into a room. When our calls became shorter, then rare, then gone.

We didn't break. We faded.

And that's the hardest kind of ending the one without a moment to hold onto. No slammed doors. No closure. Just... the quiet realization that something once so full is now empty.

If I had known that was the last time you'd call me "mine," I would've held it longer.
If I had known that was our last hug, I would've never let go.

But maybe that's the cruel kindness of unspoken goodbyes they don't shatter you all at once. They let you feel every crack, slowly.

Still listening for a goodbye that never came,

Muse.

You Grew Where I Broke,I never told you
how my world was weathered long before you
entered it. I was a field left fallow, riddled
with cracks, and afraid that even the slightest
seed would fall through and die. Then you
came soft rain after a drought your presence
coaxing petals from my bruised heart.

Loving you made me face the fissures I'd
hidden so carefully. Each time you laughed, I
felt new roots twisting inside me, unknotting
old fears. When you leaned in to listen to my
silences, I realized how buried my own voice
had grown. You reached corners of me I
thought beyond repair.

I watched you bloom in warm sunlight, arms
open to possibility, and thought: How did
someone so full of life find her way to
someone so worn? You taught me that love
doesn't demand perfection. It waters what it
finds, even if the soil seems impossible to till.

Though I was breaking, you were growing
undeterred by my brokenness. And in your
steadiness, I found the courage to rebuild. For
that, and so much more, I owe you everything.

Always,
Muse.

A Love Too Loud for the World,they said we
burned too brightly. Our whispers felt like
thunderclaps in quiet rooms. When you
smiled, I erupted in a thousand sparks and
some people covered their ears. We were two
hearts drumming a rhythm no one else could
hear, and sometimes I wondered if the world
was meant to handle our kind of music.

I remember the night I serenaded you on that
balcony, my voice cracking with raw longing.
Neighbors peered from their windows. Some
scowled. Others leaned out, curious. I saw
their faces morph from annoyance to intrigue
when you laughed and danced beneath the
moon.

We lived on the edge of "too much." Our love
was a wildfire beautiful, dangerous, and
impossible to contain. Yet in your arms, I
found that fire's warmth was all I ever
wanted. Each embrace was an anthem, each
kiss a declaration: you and I against the quiet.

Let them talk. Let them step back. We knew what it meant to roar, to feel every beat rushing through our veins. Our love was never meant to whisper it was always meant to resound.

Yours in every crescendo,
Muse.

In the Spaces You Didn't Fill,there were spaces between us silent corridors in my soul you never walked through. We shared so much: laughter, dreams, secrets. Yet some rooms remained locked, the keys lost long before you arrived. I wrote you into my joy but left out the shadowed parts I feared you couldn't carry.

I wonder if you ever sensed that pull my half-offered hand, my lingering glance at memories I hadn't shared. I hid the darkest chapters of my past, thinking I protected you. Instead, I protected myself from the risk that you might turn away.

In those empty corners, loneliness echoed. I longed for you to fill every inch of me, but the doors were shut. I yearned for you to know the chapters I couldn't speak, but I chose silence. And in that silence, regret took root.

Today I write to say I'm sorry for the walls I built. I wish I had trusted you more, shown you the full landscape of my heart. Perhaps then, our love would have been a home complete, unafraid of the dark.

With quiet longing,
Muse.

I Wrote You in Present Tense,even now I speak of you as though you're beside me. I write letters that drift unanswered, paper boats set loose on a river that no longer runs toward you. My mind refuses to accept that you have become a memory, that our late-night conversations now echo only in my head.

Last night I told someone about your new favorite show as if you'd just told me yourself. I described your laugh the way it falls between a sigh and a song then caught myself. You're not there to correct me, to roll your eyes and toss popcorn at me from across the couch.

I find your belongings still nestled in the corners of my apartment: your coffee mug, the scarf you left on the back of the chair. Each item is a ghost that breathes your presence back into my days. I set the table for two out of habit, and only when the second plate goes untouched do I remember to push it aside.

I write to you in present tense because I'm not ready to let go of the "we" that once was. If I stayed frozen here long enough, maybe time would circle back and bring you home.

Holding onto hope (or holding onto you),
Muse.

The Bloom and the Wither I want to thank you, first, for allowing me the privilege of witnessing your bloom. You turned your face to every ray of light life offered, teaching me to search for brightness in my own dark skies. I saw you grow stronger, petals unfurling in glorious defiance of every storm.

But as seasons shift, so must we. Even the sturdiest sunflower eventually bows its head. Our love, explosive and beautiful, met its own twilight. The wind that once carried our laughter also sowed seeds of doubt: Was my fear of losing you repelling you? Did my walls narrow your sky?

I choose to remember the bloom the warmth that radiated from you, the hope you planted deep in me. And I choose to accept the wither not as failure, but as part of our cycle. Life grants no perpetual spring. Healing, too, has seasons.

So here I stand, petals drifting in the autumn air, grateful for every moment under your sun. May you find new light wherever you go, and may I learn to shine again, even as the days grow shorter.

With love everlasting,
Muse.

When Memories Became Thorns,there was a time when memories of you were soft they warmed my chest like morning sun. But now, they pierce. The same flashbacks that used to make me smile now arrive like splinters beneath my skin.

I hear your voice in songs I used to love, and I flinch. I walk past your old café and turn away.

Even your name once my favorite word now echoes like a wound.

I didn't realize memories could betray me. That moments once cherished could feel like minefields. But that's what grief does it turns joy into ache, turns love into something sharp.

And yet, I hold onto these thorns. Not because I enjoy the pain, but because even hurting reminds me you were once real. You mattered. We mattered.

Maybe someday these thorns will bloom again. But for now, I bleed.

Still remembering,
Muse.

The Ache of Almosts

We almost made it.
Almost moved in together.
Almost planned that trip.
Almost said forever without trembling.

But "almost" is the cruelest kind of grief it leaves no closure. Just open doors in empty rooms.

I still imagine what we could have been. I see us old and grey, bickering in a kitchen full of spices and jazz music. I see you in a dress you never wore, reading vows we never wrote. I see it all the parallel universe where we made it.

And then I open my eyes.
And it's just me.
Just silence.

You taught me how deep the ache of "almost" can run not just in the heart, but in the bones.

And maybe, just maybe, that ache is love trying to stay alive.

Forever caught in the almost,
Muse.

How Do You Mourn Someone Still Breathing? You're still out there laughing, living, breathing and yet I grieve you like the dead.
Isn't that the strangest thing? Mourning someone who still exists, just... not in your world anymore?

You haunt my mornings. Not with ghosts, but with silence. Not with shadows, but with absence. I see pictures of you with strangers, and it feels like betrayal, even though we made no promises anymore.

I wonder if you think of me. If my name still holds any weight in your world. Or if I've faded into background noise another song you once loved but no longer play.

This is a grief without funerals.
No flowers. No condolences.
Just me, walking through the ruins of a love that still echoes, even as the city around it has moved on.

How do I let go of someone who's still breathing?

Still aching,
Muse.

Unloving You, Gently,I thought unloving you would require violence tearing you out of my heart like a thorn, burning your name from my memory. But it didn't happen like that. It happened in small ways. Quiet ways.

One day, I stopped checking your profile.
Another, I stopped rehearsing things I'd say if
we met again.
Then one night, I fell asleep without your
name on my mind.

Unloving you wasn't a war. It was surrender.
And that made it harder.

You deserved to be remembered loudly. But
instead, I'm learning to let you go in whispers.
Not because you weren't everything but
because I need to become something again.

You were home once.
Now I must learn to be home to myself.

With soft hands, I'm putting you down.

Gently,
Muse.

Silence in the Shape of Her Name,
My Beloved there's a kind of silence that
speaks louder than words the silence after
love ends. It's not the silence of peace. It's the
silence of things unsaid, of truths we couldn't
bear to voice.

I carry your name like a sacred secret now. I don't speak it often. But when I do even just in thought it still rings with longing. Your name isn't just a name. It's a place I lived in, once. A scent, a season, a sigh.

When I say your name, the air changes. It turns into autumn. Into dusk. Into memories too delicate to touch.

This silence, it has your shape.
And maybe that's all grief really is:
The space where your presence used to live.

Still holding your echo,
Muse.

I Learned to Hold Myself Again

Dear Self,
I used to think love meant someone else holding me together. That healing had to come

from their voice, their hands, their presence.
But when they left, I realized: I was still here.

It began small brushing my teeth without
breaking. Making my bed. Taking a walk.
Choosing silence not because I was lonely, but
because it gave me peace.

I stopped waiting to be rescued.
Started showing up for myself.
It wasn't glamorous. It was messy and quiet
and real.

And little by little, I remembered how to hold
my own hand. How to sit with my own storms.
How to be proud of myself, even on the days I
barely survived.

This is what growth feels like not loud, not
fast. But steady. And mine.

Always becoming,
Muse.

Peace Isn't Loud

Dear Me,

I used to think peace had to look like joy loud laughter, bright mornings, the kind of sunshine that dances. But peace isn't always loud.

Sometimes, it's silence that doesn't sting.
It's making tea and not crying when no one texts.
It's watching the rain and not feeling like something's missing.

Peace is not about the absence of grief. It's about learning to carry it without letting it crush you.
It's choosing not to fight every thought.
Letting go of what you thought should've been, and resting in what is.

I used to chase happiness like a storm. Now, I wait for peace like a soft wind. And when it comes, I sit with it. Grateful. Gentle. Still.

May it stay a little longer this time.

Quietly yours,
Muse.

Love Letters I Wrote for Myself

Dear Muse

You are not too much.
You are not too sensitive.
You are not broken beyond repair.

I used to write letters for others to win them,
to keep them, to explain myself. But now, I
write them for me.

To remind myself of the days I didn't give up.
To celebrate the nights I let go without
answers.
To honour the way I showed up for myself,
even when it hurt.

You deserve the same love you gave.
You deserve softness, even when no one else
sees your struggle.
You deserve to rest without guilt, to speak
without shrinking, to breathe without
apology.

You are worthy not because someone stayed,
but because you did.

With deepest love,
Muse.

Becoming the Safe Place I Craved
Dear Me,

I kept looking for a home in people.
But they were not houses they were travelers,
just like me.

It took losing almost everything to realize that
I could become my own shelter. That I could
be the calm after my own storms. The arms I
longed for were always mine.

Now, I talk to myself gently. I check in. I set
boundaries not to push others away, but to
keep my peace close.

I'm not perfect. Some days I still ache. But I no
longer run from it I sit with it like an old
friend. Because I know now: the hurt doesn't
define me. My healing does.

And in this soft rebuilding, I have finally
become the safe place I was always searching
for.

Rooted,
Muse

I Loved Her, But I Chose Me, I will always love you not in the way that expects return, but in the quiet remembrance of what we shared.

But I have finally chosen me.
I choose mornings that don't begin with wondering if you miss me.
I choose nights that end with peace, not panic.
I choose a heart that still believes in love, but no longer begs for it.

You were my favorite chapter.
But this this is the part where I become the author again.

And I am writing something new now.
Something healing.
Something whole.

You were once everything.
But now, I am.

With love, without need,
Muse.

I Didn't Mean to Be Distant

Dear Muse

There were nights I saw you watching
me eyes full of questions you never asked out
loud. I felt your worry, your love, your
confusion.

I wasn't trying to disappear. I was trying to
hold myself together.

Sometimes, I felt like I was drowning in your
tenderness. Not because it wasn't beautiful
but because I didn't know how to receive it
without feeling like I was taking more than I
could give.

You looked at me like I was poetry.
But some days, I didn't even feel like words.

I Loved You Quietly,
You loved me out loud with gestures, words,
and presence.
I loved you in the quiet ways:
In the way I memorized your coffee order.
In the way I made space for your thoughts,
even when they tangled.
In how I chose not to leave, even when I was
afraid of staying.

You didn't always notice.
And I didn't always show it right.
But I loved you. God, I did.
Just... differently.

I Felt Like I Was Fading,
There was a version of myself I wanted to
be someone whole, present, unshaken. But
each time I tried to meet you in your depth, I
found myself unraveling.

You were fire and I was flicker.
And I didn't know how to tell you that loving
you made me feel more alive and more lost at
the same time.

It wasn't your fault.
You were steady. You were everything.
But I wasn't ready to be seen the way you saw
me.

So I faded.
Quietly.
Painfully.
Out of love not because I didn't feel it, but
because I didn't know how to hold it.

I Heard Every Silence Too,
You think I didn't notice the silence growing
between us but I did. I felt it every time you
hesitated before saying "I love you." Every
time your laughter didn't reach your eyes.

You weren't the only one hurting.
I just got better at pretending I wasn't.

There were days I wanted to reach for you, to
tell you I missed us but by then, it felt like we
were both already halfway out the door.

Maybe neither of us knew how to stay.
Maybe we both hoped the other would pull us
back.

I Still Think of You,
I don't know if I deserve to say this.
But sometimes, I still whisper your name into
the pillow.
Sometimes I find songs you'd love, and I
wonder if you've heard them.
Sometimes, I pass places we went to and I
pause, just for a moment.

You're not just a memory, Muse.
You're a mark.
And no matter how far I've gone,
a part of me still lives in the way you loved
me.

If you ever wonder whether you mattered
You did.
You always will.
Sunflower

The Love We Tried to Hold
We Were Almost Everything,
We weren't just two people in love
we were two stories trying to be written in
the same book, on the same page,
but with hands that trembled differently.

I think about how we started
how we moved from silence to softness, from
glances to laughter,
and how quickly we built something out of
nothing.

It felt right, didn't it?
Like two puzzle pieces trying to remember
they once fit.

But sometimes, even love gets tired.
Even magic needs rest.
And I think we burned so brightly at the start,
we didn't see we were setting ourselves on
fire.

I still carry the ashes not with regret,
but with reverence.

The Things We Never Said,
There were so many times I wanted to ask,
"Are you still here, or just afraid to leave?"

But I didn't.
Because I was afraid the answer would undo
me.

You stopped asking how my day was.
I stopped asking what you were thinking.
We danced around the truth with small talk
and smiles,
afraid that honesty might break us.

I wonder what would've happened
if we had just told the truth sooner.
Maybe we could've saved us.
Or maybe we would've at least known
what we were trying to save.

Now the silence between us echoes louder
than anything we ever said.

Holding You While Losing You
I held your hand through quiet storms,
watched you drift into your thoughts,
trying to anchor you with my presence
while feeling the tide pull you away.

There is no pain like watching the person you
love
become a stranger slowly
not by betrayal,
but by becoming unreachable.

I kept holding on,
tightening my grip with every moment you
slipped further,
hoping you'd notice,
hoping you'd return.

But you were already elsewhere,
wrapped in your own silence,
carrying burdens I wasn't allowed to touch.

Loving you began to feel like trying to hold
water

and even when I was soaked in memories,
my hands were still empty.

The Apologies We Owe Each Other
 I owe you an apology
for expecting you to be whole when you were
hurting.

You owe me one
for pretending you were fine when you
weren't.

We both owe each other
a conversation we never had
one where we sit in the mess,
look each other in the eyes,
and finally say what our hearts were
screaming
in all that silence.

But maybe we ran out of time.
Or maybe we were both too exhausted
to keep trying to explain ourselves to
someone
we used to feel understood by.

And so, we just let go.

Without closure.

Without clarity.
Just the quiet ache
of almost.

What We Left Behind
I still have your hoodie.
 It smells like you on cold mornings
like warmth I can't reach anymore.

I still have screenshots of our texts,
inside jokes I can't share with anyone else,
and photos that feel like they belong to
someone else's life now.

I left parts of myself in your laugh,
in your kitchen,
in the way you said my name.

And you left echoes of yourself in every place
we touched
my playlists, my habits, my dreams.

What we built might be over,
but what we became in those moments
that lingers.

Even in endings,

love leaves fingerprints.

After You Left, I Stayed With Myself,
The night you finally became memory
I didn't cry.
I just sat
staring at the walls you once leaned on,
listening to the silence that used to hold your
laugh.

The air felt different.
I felt different.

It wasn't dramatic. It wasn't cinematic.
It was just... real.

I was alone again
but this time, it wasn't loneliness that haunted
me.
It was all the versions of me I had neglected
while chasing the idea of us.

So I stayed.
With myself.
For the first time in a long time.

The Mirror and the Mess,

I started cleaning my room one Sunday.
Not for the sake of order
but because I needed to feel in control of
something.

I found old notes,
a ticket from that movie we loved,
a photo you once tucked into my journal.

And then I looked in the mirror.

Really looked.

There I was
bruised but breathing,
hurting but whole,
a little lost but finally grounded in truth.

Healing didn't come all at once.
It came in small rituals:
Getting out of bed.
Brushing my teeth.
Not reaching for my phone to see if you
messaged.

Each act was a quiet rebellion
against the part of me that still waited for you.

The Days I Didn't Think of You, I used to
wonder if healing meant forgetting.
But it doesn't.
Healing meant learning to live
without the constant ache of your name.

There were days I thought of you so much,
I could feel your shadow beside me.

And then,
there were days you didn't come to mind
not in the morning,
not even in the music.

And on those days,
I felt guilty at first.
Like I was betraying something sacred.

But with time,
I realized forgetting wasn't the goal.
Peace was.

And peace sounds like silence
but without sorrow.

When I Loved Myself Enough to Let Go
I kept holding onto our story,

like a book with missing pages
hoping one day it would make sense.

But I finally understood
you don't need to understand every ending
to move on from it.

I loved you.
Fully.
Messily.
Beautifully.

But now I love myself
enough to admit
that I deserve someone who doesn't have to
wrestle with the thought of staying.

And maybe one day,
when our ghosts pass each other in the places
we once called ours,
they'll smile
knowing we tried.

But now, I choose peace.

And peace means letting go.

Thank You for Breaking Me Open,

I no longer write about you with a bleeding
pen.
I write with gratitude.

You broke me open
and in the wreckage,
I met myself.

You taught me the depth of love,
but also the danger of losing yourself in it.

You taught me that silence can be a language,
but healing must be a choice.

I won't pretend it didn't hurt.
It did.
But pain made way for truth.

And truth is:
I needed to lose you
to finally come home to myself.

So thank you
for being the fire,
for being the lesson,
for being the poem I had to live
before I could write again.

The Letter I Never Sent

This letter isn't for fixing things.
It's for freeing them.

I won't beg you to come back.
I won't ask for explanations.
I just want you to know:

I forgive you.

Not because you asked for it
but because I no longer want to carry this
weight in my chest.

We both loved the best way we knew how.
Sometimes that love wasn't enough.
And that's okay now.

If you ever think of me,
I hope it's with a softness.

Because that's how I think of you.

Loving Doesn't Always Mean Keeping

I used to think that if I truly loved someone,
I had to hold on.
 But I was wrong.

Sometimes, the greatest form of love
is release.

Letting go of what no longer fits.
Letting someone become who they need to be
even if it's far away from you.

I didn't lose you.
I just stopped needing to own you.

Love doesn't end when it leaves.
It echoes.
It changes form.
And then it teaches us how to begin again.

When the Silence Became Peaceful
For so long, silence reminded me of you.
Of distance. Of endings.
Of things unsaid.

But now, silence feels like sunrise.
It feels like breathing.
It feels like standing at the edge of the ocean
not to drown, but to feel alive again.

I no longer fear quiet rooms.

They've become my sanctuary.

Where once I searched for your voice,
I now listen for my own.

And I hear it clearly.

I Am Becoming,
Every scar tells a story
and mine sings of survival.

I am no longer the version of me
who begged for love to stay.

I am the version who stayed with himself
when love walked away.

I've learned to laugh again
not just politely,
but with a fullness that shakes the sky.

I've learned to be gentle with myself,
to take long walks without waiting for
someone to join me,
to dream again not of "us,"
but of *me*.

I am becoming.
And it's beautiful.

If We Ever Meet Again
If one day you find me in a crowded room
laughing, shining,
arms wrapped in something new
I hope you smile.

Not because you still love me,
but because you're proud.

And if you've healed too,
I'll smile back.

We don't have to speak.
We don't have to explain.

Just two people
who once held each other,
now holding peace.

To the One Who Reads Between My Lines
If you made it this far,
thank you.

For sitting with me in the ache.
For honoring the quiet spaces.
For feeling the words I could barely speak.

This book is not just about her.
It's about you.
Me.
Us.

The ones who loved deeply.
Who lost quietly.
Who healed slowly.

You are not alone.

"To the Over-thinkers"

"To the overthinkers
those who live in their heads,
feel too deeply,
and love like it's the last thing they'll ever do...

You are not too much.
You are not too fragile.
You are a galaxy of thought,
wrapped in human skin.

You cry when others don't.
You stay when others run.
You notice the cracks
and call them art.

You have been misunderstood
labeled as complicated,
called intense.

But I see you.

And I promise
there is a softness waiting
on the other side of this storm.

Keep loving.
Keep writing.
Keep breathing, even when it hurts.

Because somewhere in the silence,
you'll find yourself again.

And this time,
you'll stay."

Chapter 2-*Reunion and Healing*

I Thought You Didn't See Me,
I thought you didn't see me in the club.
My heart was racing,
I was so happy to see your face again.
I thought I healed.
I just saw you at night,
but you did brighten my day.
I never thought you would reach out to me
ever again.
I had been doubting myself
debating if I should text you,
just to see how you've been.
Doubt kills, I see that now.
One of the days,
I found myself reminiscing about you
how I was first drawn to your beauty,
not knowing the real beauty
was buried deeper inside you.
The day you accepted to be my better half
was the day you changed me
how I carried myself in this world,
how I viewed love,
how I loved myself.
Loving you
was the best thing that ever happened to me.
You brought love and happiness.
You brought comfort and light
in my darkest hours.
You held me when life had me down.

If it were up to me,
I would have made you my wife.
1. I Didn't Mean to Be DistantDear Muse
There were nights I saw you watching me out
loud. I felt your worry, your love, your
confusion.
eyes full of questions you never asked
I wasn't trying to disappear. I was trying to
hold myself together.
Sometimes, I felt like I was drowning in your
tenderness. Not because it wasn't
beautiful but because I didn't know how to
receive it without feeling like I was
taking more than I could give.
You looked at me like I was poetry.
But some days, I didn't even feel like words.

I Loved You Quietly
You loved me out loud with gestures, words,
and presence.
I loved you in the quiet ways:
In the way I memorized your coffee order.
In the way I made space for your thoughts,
even when they tangled.
In how I chose not to leave, even when I was
afraid of staying.
You didn't always notice.
And I didn't always show it right.
But I loved you. God, I did.

Just... differently.

I Felt Like I Was Fading
There was a version of myself I wanted to be
someone whole, present, unshaken.
But each time I tried to meet you in your
depth, I found myself unraveling.
You were fire and I was flicker.
And I didn't know how to tell you that loving
you made me feel more alive and
more lost at the same time.
It wasn't your fault.
You were steady. You were everything.
But I wasn't ready to be seen the way you saw
me.
So I faded.
Quietly.Painfully.
Out of love not because I didn't feel it, but
because I didn't know how to hold it.

But I Heard Every Silence Too
You think I didn't notice the silence growing
between us but I did. I felt it every
time you hesitated before saying "I love you."
Every time your laughter didn't
reach your eyes.
You weren't the only one hurting.
I just got better at pretending I wasn't.

There were days I wanted to reach for you, to tell you I missed us but by then, it
felt like we were both already halfway out the door.
Maybe neither of us knew how to stay.
Maybe we both hoped the other would pull us back.

I Still Think of You
I don't know if I deserve to say this.
But sometimes, I still whisper your name into the pillow.
Sometimes I find songs you'd love, and I wonder if you've heard them.
Sometimes, I pass places we went to and I pause, just for a moment.
You're not just a memory, T.
You're a mark.
And no matter how far I've gone,
a part of me still lives in the way you loved me.
If you ever wonder whether you mattered
You did.
You always will.

The Night We Didn't Speak
I couldn't sleep that night.
I kept replaying your face in my mind.

Your laughter,your smile when you were with
your friends,
and that one moment
when I think you saw me too.
But neither of us said a word.
I stood there,
watching you through smoke,
flashing lights,
and blurry memories.
So much I wanted to say.
So much I rehearsed,
but the moment felt fragile
like if I touched it,
it would disappear.
I wondered if your heart raced like mine.
Or maybe you've mastered the art of letting go
better than I ever could.
I asked myself,
Would she even want to talk to me?
Does she still remember our quiet mornings,
the playlists,
the long walks,
the late-night calls that saved us both?
You were right there,
yet miles away.
And I was drowning in silence
my favorite place
before it started echoing your name.
The world danced around me,

but I was frozen in time.
Because seeing you again
felt like both a gift
and a wound reopened.
And still,
we didn't speak.

The Life I Built Without YouAfter you left,
the days were quiet.
Too quiet.
Even the city seemed to move slower
without you in it.
I threw myself into work.
9 to 5s became 7 to 9s.
Weekends blurred into weekdays,
and everything I once loved
felt like something you touched
so I avoided it.
I stopped listening to certain songs.
I stopped going to places we used to love.
Even coffee didn't taste the same.
I found peace in routine.
In doing what needed to be done.
Eat. Work. Sleep. Repeat.
It was the only way I could keep from
drowning
in the memories I couldn't delete.
People said I looked "better,"
but they never saw the parts of me

still whispering your name
at 2AM.
I dated.
But no one made me feel like you did.
No one saw me
like you did.
No one stayed.
The life I built without you
was functional.
Neat.
Safe.
But it lacked the chaos of love,
the softness of shared silence,
the comfort of someone who just gets you
without trying.
And as strong as I've become,I won't lie
part of me still wonders
what life would have looked like
if you stayed.
If we stayed.
But instead,
I learned how to be alone.
How to hold myself
the way you used to hold me.
How to forgive myself
for letting go too soon
or too late.
This is the life I built without you
stable,

quiet,
and almost whole.
But still missing
something I can't replace.

Writing You in Every Verse
I tried writing about other things.
Sunrises.
Growth.
Peace.
Even joy.
But somehow,
your shadow always slipped into the page.
You were in every metaphor I crafted,
in every silence between stanzas,
in every note I hummed
when no one else was listening.
I thought I was over you,
but my pen knew better.
It kept bleeding truths
I was too proud to admit.I wrote about
healing,
but you were the reason I broke.
I wrote about strength,
but it came from losing you.
I wrote about love,
but it always sounded like your name.
Funny how I swore I moved on,

yet I was still building you altars
in every poem.
Some nights,
I'd sit by the window,
headphones in,
letting a beat carry me back
to our slow dances in the kitchen,
your voice humming next to mine,
the world outside forgotten.
You were my favorite lyric.
The unsaid line I never performed.
The hook that still gets stuck in my head
every time I hear your laugh in a stranger's
voice.
They say writing helps you heal.
But I'm not sure if it healed me
or just helped me miss you
more beautifully.
I wasn't just writing stories.
I was writing you.
Over and over.
Until maybe,
just maybe,
you'd read one
and know it was always you.

I Dreamed of You Again

I dreamed of you again last night.
Your voice was soft
like the way you used to say my namewhen
the world was too loud.
You didn't speak much.
You just looked at me,
the way you used to
like I was home.
In the dream,
you wore that oversized hoodie I always
loved.
The one you said smelled like me,
even after I hadn't worn it for days.
We sat on that same bench
where we used to talk about forever.
You laughed at something I said,
and for a moment,
it felt like we had never broken.
No wounds.
No silence.
Just us.
You touched my hand
and I swear I felt it
even after I woke up.
My chest still ached
with the weight of your absence,
but I was grateful for the visit.
Even if it was only in a dream.
I've learned to live with missing you

in the daylight.
But at night,
my mind still reaches for you
without permission.
And that's the hardest part
not the dream,
but the waking.
Opening my eyes
and realizing you're still gone.
The bed still empty.
The room still quiet.And the hoodie
still folded
in the back of my closet.
Sometimes I wonder
if you ever dream of me too.
If you wake up
with my name caught between your breath
and your heart.
Or if I only live in your past now,
while you still live in every part of me.

I saw you before you saw me.
You looked... different.
Calmer.
Maybe older.
Like life had done its job of breaking you in a
little.

I don't know what I expected after all this
time,
but seeing you again brought everything back
the good,
the chaos,
the quiet.
Us.
I wanted to say something.
But I froze.
Because how do you greet the person
who once held your entire heart
like it was fragile glass?
I walked past you
like a stranger.
But my chest
my chest was loud.
Screaming your name
while my lips stayed shut.I told my friends I
was fine.
That I was over you.
That I was better now.
But they didn't see the way my hands shook
when I texted your name
and erased it before pressing send.
Truth is,
I loved you longer than I admitted.
Even after we stopped talking.
Even after you moved in silence.
You weren't perfect.

But I was scared.
Scared of needing someone too deeply.
Scared of giving all of me
and losing myself in the process.
So I left.
And every day since,
I've asked myself if I did the right thing
or if I just chose safety
over love.
I watched your life from afar.
Your music.
Your words.
And even when they weren't about me,
I felt them like they were.
You said nothing.
And I said nothing.
Two hearts pretending
they forgot how to speak.
But if I'm honest...
I never stopped hoping
you'd find your way back to me.
Or that I'd finally find the courage
to meet you halfway.
Maybe this time,
we won't let silencebe the end of our story.

I Had to Learn to Breathe Without You
I had to learn to breathe without you.

It was the kind of lesson no one teaches
how to unlove someone who never truly left
your heart.
At first, everything reminded me of you.
The songs you played.
The mug you left behind.
That one street we always took the long way
through
just to be in each other's company a little
longer.
I used to reach for my phone
to tell you about the smallest things
how the sky looked like spilled paint,
how I finally finished that book,
how I missed your voice when the world got
too loud.
But I stopped myself.
Every time.
Because silence had become our language.
And I didn't want to speak out of turn
anymore.
I blamed you at first.
For not fighting.
For letting me walk away
without asking me to stay.
But I've grown since then.
And now I know
we were both tired.
Tired of miscommunication.

Of dancing around emotions.
Of trying to be strong
when all we really wanted
was to be soft with each other again.
I cried a lot,
but I also healed.
I started writing too.Not like you
not the poetic kind.
But enough to get the heaviness out of me.
I wrote about you.
About how I hated you some days
and missed you most others.
How I wore your old shirt to sleep
just to feel close to the version of you I
couldn't reach.
I dated someone new once.
He was kind.
Gentle.
But he wasn't you.
And I hated that I compared everything good
to a love I once called home.
So I stopped.
I stopped searching for you in strangers.
Stopped hoping you'd show up in places you
weren't supposed to.
I started choosing me.
And still...
the moment I saw you again,
it all came back.

Not because I hadn't healed.
But because some people
don't get replaced
no matter how much time passes.
I don't know if we'll ever get it right.
But I know I've grown.
And if we try again,
it'll be two whole people,
not two halves looking to be saved.

I Never Stopped Writing You in My Mind
I never stopped writing you in my mind.
Even when I stopped texting.Even when I told
myself you were part of my past.
You still lived in the background
of every moment I wished you could see.
I'd walk past a sunset that looked like the kind
you used to describe,
and I'd whisper, "He would've loved this."
I'd hear a melody playing in a coffee shop,
and I'd pause
because it sounded like your type of pain
turned into beauty.
There were pieces of you
in the quietest hours of my day.
When I smiled at something no one else
noticed.

When I held in tears because I had no one to
cry to the way I cried to you.
When I laughed so hard I snorted
and remembered how you used to say
I only did that when I was truly happy.
I wonder if you ever knew
how much space you took up
even after you left.
I tried to unlove you in loud ways.
Deleting photos.
Unfollowing.
Burning letters in my journal with shaky
hands and stubborn tears.
But the love didn't leave with those things.
It just buried itself deeper
in poems,
in silences,
in glances at the sky.
You became the story I kept rewriting
without ever letting anyone read the drafts.
And the truth?
The truth is
even though I moved on,
even though I healed,
even though I built a life that didn't include
you...There was always a part of me
waiting for the day you'd look at me again
like I was still your favorite sentence
in a book you never finished reading.

Maybe love doesn't always leave.
Maybe it just changes rooms inside your heart
quieter, but still alive.
I didn't reach out,
not because I didn't care,
but because I thought you didn't.
Now that I've seen you again...
I wonder what could live
in the spaces between us now.
I'm no longer writing about missing you.
Now I'm writing about wondering
if two people who once broke apart
can still build something
honest,
and new.

If I Could Speak to You Now
If I could speak to you now,
I'd tell you that I read every word
you never said aloud
but somehow I still heard.
I don't know if you ever meant for me to feel
you again this deeply.
But I did.
I do.
You were the sentence I never stopped
rereading.
The one I never finished writing.

The echo in rooms I hadn't walked through in
years.
I wanted to reach out so many times.
I had messages typed out, unsent.
Voicemails deleted.
Dreams that ended with your nameand
mornings that began with your memory.
You weren't just love.
You were clarity.
A mirror.
A storm and a shelter all in one.
Sometimes I hated you
for moving on so gracefully
not knowing that your silence
was the loudest thing I ever heard.
I thought time would heal it.
I thought new routines,
late nights,
louder music
would drown the thoughts of you.
But nothing ever did.
I stopped chasing things
when I realized the only thing I really wanted
was peace.
And somehow,
you always felt like the definition of it.
I don't know if we could ever go back.
Maybe we're not supposed to.
But what if this is not about going back?

What if it's about choosing each other again
not out of nostalgia,
but because we're both standing here now,
wiser, softer,
and still drawn to each other
after everything?
If I could speak to you now,
I'd say:
I never stopped caring.
I never stopped praying for your light.
And if there's a space for me in your story,
I'd be honored to fill it again
with more honesty,more patience,
and more love than ever before.
But if you're okay with just silence again,
I'll respect that too.
Just know this:
You were never forgotten.
You were never just a chapter.
You were the reason I kept writing.

The Day We Finally Spoke
It was nothing like I imagined.
No grand speech.
No tears spilling onto the floor.
Just... us.
Standing in front of each other,
after everything,

like time had folded in on itself.
You looked at me
not like a stranger,
not like a ghost,
but like someone you used to pray for,
and maybe still do.
I opened my mouth first.
"Hey."
Simple.
Like we hadn't spent years
saying everything in silence.
You smiled,
and it felt like someone pressed rewind
on every heartbreak I ever wrote about you.
"I wasn't sure you'd say anything," you said.
"I wasn't sure either," I admitted.
"But I couldn't walk away again."There was a pause,
not awkward
just full.
Full of everything we didn't say before.
"I've been writing again," I added.
"I know. I read some of it," you replied.
"I always knew you'd turn pain into
something beautiful."
I looked down.
"You were always the beauty in it."
You stepped closer.

"I never stopped hoping we'd meet again. Not to start over... but to start
different."
That sentence hung in the air.
Unrushed.
Honest.
I nodded,
still unsure of what the future held,
but certain about this moment.
"I don't know what this means for us," I said.
"But I'm here."
You took a breath.
"Me too."
And that was it.
Not a promise.
Not a fantasy.
Just presence.
Two people,
finally ready to speak,
after learning the weight of silence.

Relearning Each OtherWe didn't fall back in
love in a day.
We didn't even try to.
Instead,
we started with quiet conversations
over coffee and park benches.
Talking like friends
who'd once held hands through storms.

You told me about your new routines
early mornings, journaling,
the little bakery you found on Sundays.
I told you about my writing
how I stopped rhyming pain
and started writing healing.
How I still carried pieces of you
between the verses.
There were pauses.
Moments we didn't know what to say.
Moments we remembered
how easy it was to get lost in each other.
But this time,
we didn't rush.
We didn't force closure
or chase a happy ending.
We asked questions:
How are you, really?
What are you afraid of now?
Do you still believe in forever?
We sat in rooms with open windows,
letting old air escape.
We cried sometimes.
We laughed unexpectedly.
And slowly,
we started learning new things:
The way you liked your tea now.
The songs I play when I miss home.

The way your voice softenswhen you speak
about healing.
It wasn't perfect.
But it was real.
Two people with scarred hearts
trying to build something softer
out of everything that once broke them.
You told me one evening,
"I don't want what we had before.
I want what we can be now."
I smiled.
Because that was all I wanted too.
Not the version of us from the past,
but the version of us
who survived the silence
and still chose to speak.

The Song We Never Finished
There was a melody we started years ago.
Just a few chords,
some lines scribbled in your notebook,
a voice memo I kept
even after we stopped speaking.
I found it the other night.
Hidden between old files
and forgotten dreams.
I sent it to you with a short message:
"Do you remember this?"

Minutes later,
three dots appeared.
Then you replied:
"Of course. I never stopped humming it."
So we met.
In a small studio.
Nothing fancy.
Just your guitar,my pen,
and our unfinished past
resting quietly between us.
You played the old chords.
I filled in new words.
You hummed a verse.
I smiled.
I remembered that hum
the one you used to sing
when you were nervous but hopeful.
We didn't talk about the old version of us.
We just stayed in the music.
That was always our language anyway.
It was healing
watching us build something
instead of breaking things down again.
No blaming.
No old wounds ripped open.
Just sound.
And presence.
The chorus came from you this time.
Simple.

Raw.
Real.
"We didn't make it back,
but we found our way here.
And maybe here
is enough for now."
When we finished recording,
you looked at me like you used to
but softer.
Like someone who knows my ruins
but chooses to stay anyway.
"I'm proud of us," you said.
Not "I love you."
Not yet.But it held just as much weight.
I nodded,
because I was proud too.
Of how we let time do its work.
Of how we didn't rush healing.
Of how we turned silence
into a song.

When You Finally Said It
It was after the release.
The song went live at midnight.
By morning,
our inboxes were flooded
messages from strangers who felt seen,
from friends who didn't know

we still spoke,
from ourselves
finally listening.
But none of it compared
to the moment that followed.
We were in your car,
parked outside your apartment,
windows slightly cracked,
letting in the evening air
and the sound of our own silence.
I was staring ahead,
hands fidgeting in my lap,
when you turned to me and said:
"I still love you."
Just like that.
No warning.
No dramatic lead-up.
Like it had been waiting
at the tip of your tongue
for too long.I didn't speak.
Not right away.
Because my heart was too loud
to hear my thoughts clearly.
You continued:
"Not in the same way as before.
Not in a desperate, fix-me way.
But in a quiet, steady way.
The kind of love that grew
even when I wasn't sure I'd see you again."

And I looked at you
not with surprise,
but with recognition.
Because I'd been carrying the same words
like unopened letters
inside my chest.
"I still love you too," I whispered.
"But I want to do it right this time.
With no half-love.
No hiding.
Just... honesty."
You nodded.
And for once,
it didn't feel like the start of a new chapter.
It felt like the continuation
of a love that never ended
just paused,
rewritten,
and returned softer.

When the Past Returned
It was a normal Wednesday.
We were at a small café
your favorite spot tucked between the
bookstore
and that old record shop
we used to go tobefore everything fell apart.
You were mid-sentence,

smiling at something you read,
when your face dropped.
I turned to see what caused it.
It was him.
Someone from my past.
A name you never liked,
a face you didn't trust,
a chapter you tried to forget
when you were learning how to breathe again.
He saw me.
Nodded.
Then walked over with the kind of confidence
only people with unfinished stories carry.
"Hey, man. Long time."
I stood up.
Polite. Guarded.
"Yeah. Long time."
He glanced at you.
Hesitated.
Then said,
"Didn't expect to see you two… back together."
The silence between us was instant.
Sharp.
You didn't speak.
You just picked up your cup,
sipped,
and waited for the moment to pass.
But it didn't.
Not really.

When we got home,
you sat on the edge of the bed,your back
turned to me.
"It's not about him," you said.
"It's what he represents."
And I knew what you meant.
Old pain.
Doubt.
That version of me
who chose silence
when he should've fought for you.
I knelt beside you.
No defense.
Just truth.
"I'm not him anymore.
But I know that's not enough.
So I'll prove it every day,
not with words,
but with presence."
You finally looked at me.
"I want to believe that."
And I whispered,
"Then let me make it undeniable."
Because healing isn't about pretending the
past never happened.
It's about choosing
again and again
not to return to it.

A Weekend Away
We needed air.
Space from the city,
from stares,
from questions that kept following us home.
So we packed light.
Just two bags,one playlist,
and a map that didn't really matter
because anywhere with you
felt like somewhere I wanted to be.
The drive was quiet at first.
The kind of quiet that holds things.
Old conversations,
unspoken worries,
moments too fragile for noise.
Then your voice broke through:
"Do you remember that one road trip we took...
before everything changed?"
I smiled.
"Yeah.
We played the same five songs
until we memorized each other's laughs."
You laughed again.
The same way you did then.
And I realized that maybe
we weren't trying to get back to how it was
maybe we were building something new

with the same souls.
The cabin was small.
Wooden walls,
a fireplace,
no Wi-Fi.
Just the sound of wind,
our breath,
and music we sang off-key together.
We cooked one-pan meals.
Danced in mismatched socks.
Watched the fire burn low
while talking about things that didn't need
fixing.
And for once,
nothing was heavy.
You rested your head on my chest
like the world couldn't touch us here.And I
knew
this was a new chapter.
Not a rewrite.
A rebirth.
Before we left,
we stood by the lake,
watching the sun climb out of the fog.
You looked at me,
took my hand,
and said:
"I'm still scared.
But I'm here."

And I answered,
"So am I.
And that's enough."

The Stillness Between Us
There was no dramatic moment.
No storm.
No tearful declarations.
Just a quiet evening
on the balcony of your apartment,
watching the city breathe beneath us.
You brought out two mugs.
Chamomile for you.
Mint for me.
Like always.
We didn't talk much that night.
We didn't need to.
Your head rested on my shoulder,
your hand found mine,
and in that silence
everything made sense.It wasn't about fixing
anymore.
It wasn't about proving
who was right,
or who held on longer.
It was about now.
About this heartbeat,
this night,

this version of us
that chose to stay.
You looked up and said,
"I don't know where life will take us...
but I want to walk it slowly this time."
And I nodded.
"One breath at a time."
No expectations.
No fairy tale.
Just reality wrapped in honesty,
softened by love.
It took us years,
pain,
distance,
letters unsent
and music written in heartbreak
to get here.
But here we were.
Not perfect.
Not new.
But real.
And that was enough.

The Last Letter
To the one who stayed, even when you left
I don't know how many versions of me you've
met.
The boy who didn't know how to speak,

The man who buried himself in silence,
The artist who only knew how to write when
it hurt.You've seen them all.
You loved them all.
And maybe that's what scared me.
You saw me
when I didn't even know who that was yet.
I used to think love was fireworks and loud
moments.
But you taught me
that love is in the showing up.
In the way you refilled my cup without asking,
waited for my storms to pass,
and still chose me
even when I couldn't choose myself.
There were nights I almost texted you.
Typed it all out
how much I missed you,
how I replayed your laugh in every song,
how I looked for your eyes in crowds
I didn't belong in.
But I was afraid.
Not of you
but of the truth.
That maybe love like ours
wasn't meant to come back.
And then you did.
Not as a memory,
not as a ghost,

but real.
Present.
Breathing.
I won't make promises I can't keep.
But I can give you this:
My heart,
unrushed.
My words,
honest.
My presence,consistent.
I want the slow mornings with you.
The shared playlists, the silence,
the healing.
If this is the second chance we never thought
we'd get
I'm not wasting it.
Yours, still,
and again
Me.
To the One Who Returned Softly
We met in noise,
loved in silence,
broke in echoes
we couldn't silence fast enough.
Time didn't heal
it revealed.
Taught us that absence
wasn't distance,
just space

to become.
I carried your name
in playlists,
in journal pages,
in the pauses between dreams.
You were a melody
I never stopped humming,
even when I swore
I'd forgotten the tune.
And now
you return.
Not to fix,
but to hold.
Not to rewrite,
but to rereadwhat we once abandoned.
You smile with your eyes now.
Slower.
Wiser.
And I do too.
This love
it doesn't beg for attention anymore.
It just breathes.
Like us.
Still here.
Still soft.
Still choosing.
Not because we had to.
But because
even after all the noise…

we always came back
to the silence.

Chapter 3-*Growth, Proposal, and Wedding*

The Life We Chose
Two years ago, we decided to try again not
blindly, not out of nostalgia, but with
full hearts and open hands.
The life we chose wasn't glamorous.
It didn't start with fireworks or fairytales.
It started with honesty.
With healing.
With packing our past into boxes and
unpacking hope in a one-bedroom
apartment with creaky floors and afternoon
sun that kissed our couch just right.
We didn't have it all figured out, but we had a
vision a shared rhythm, like a song
only we could hear.
You'd wake up early to water the plants.
I'd stay up late finishing edits and mixing
tracks, headphones half-off, always
half-listening in case you called my name.

We built a business together not just to make
money, but to make meaning.
Late nights, client calls, invoices, tears.
But we were never chasing status just
freedom.
Freedom to love each other without pressure.
Freedom to be soft without losing strength.
Freedom to rest in each other's arms without
fear of being too much.There were moments
we doubted it.
Fights over finances.
Silent dinners.
sounded.
That one week you slept facing the wall, and I
almost forgot how your laughter
But we kept showing up.
Choosing each other.
Day after day.
They don't tell you how real love is made not
found, not fallen into made.
In the quiet moments when no one's
watching.
In the forgiveness that comes without an
apology.
In the small gestures a mug of tea, a playlist
left playing, a note on the fridge that
just said:
"I'm proud of you. Even when you're tired.
Even when you feel like you're

failing."
We didn't find perfection.
We found peace.
And that's the life we chose.

New Silence, New Home
There's a silence that feels like distance.
Then there's a silence that feels like peace.
Ours became the second kind.
The move wasn't loud or dramatic.
No fancy moving trucks.
Just borrowed boxes, borrowed time, and two
people finally ready to plant roots.
It was a small place
white walls, unfinished wooden floors,
a kitchen where we bumped hips and shared
spoons,
a living room that doubled as a studio and a
sanctuary.
We called it home before the furniture even
arrived.
The first night, we slept on a mattress on the
floor. Your arm under my neck, the air smelled
like paint and possibility.
We ordered takeout, forgot where we packed
the forks, and ended up eating
noodles with chopsticks from the last place
we traveled to.

And I remember thinking:
This is it.
Not the moment they write about in
magazines or movies
but the one you write about in your heart.
The one that changes everything without
needing fireworks.
You taught me that home wasn't just a place.
It was in your presence.
It was in the way your voice softened when
you were proud of me.
In how you hummed when cooking.
In how your hand always reached for mine
when I overthought out loud.
The silence in this new home was different.
It didn't echo with the ghosts of past mistakes.
It didn't ache like it used to.
It rested.
It healed.
We started placing pieces of ourselves
everywhere
poems on the fridge,
your old guitar leaning by the balcony,
our vision board above the bed:
"Build something that feels like both of us."
And slowly, we did.
We turned morning coffee into rituals.
We turned fights into lessons.
We turned small wins into celebrations.

And in between all that,
we fell in love again.
Not the dizzying kind.
The grounded kind.
The kind that lets you rest.
The kind that makes you better.
The kind that finally, finally, feels like home.

The Letter I Never Gave You I wrote it on a
cold Wednesday night,
in a coffee shop two blocks from our old spot.
The city was loud, but inside me
everything was quiet.
I stared at the screen.
Then at the empty page.
Then I just... wrote.
Dear You,
If you're reading this,
it means I still care.
It means part of me hasn't healed,
and maybe never will.
There's no one to blame here.
Just timing.
Just choices.
Just silence stretched too long between two
people
who once knew how to speak without words.
I don't know when we started drifting.

Maybe it was in the little ways
me staying late,
you falling asleep before I got home,
texts that turned into read receipts with no
reply.
I hated how normal it started to feel,
not hearing you laugh.
Not seeing your eyes light up
when you talked about the future.
I hated that we got too tired to fight for each
other.
But still
you were my favorite chapter.
You were the verse I kept reciting
even after the poem ended.
There were nights I almost called.
Mornings I drafted texts and deleted them.
Birthdays where I lit a candle for you
even if you weren't mine to celebrate
anymore.And if you ever felt unloved
I'm sorry.
You were the softest thing I'd ever known,
and I got too hard trying to protect myself.
I built walls,
when I should've been building bridges to
reach you.
Maybe this letter will stay unsent.
Maybe it's just therapy on paper.
But if by some miracle it does find you...

I want you to know:
You changed me.
You softened the edges of a broken man.
You taught me how to love like it was safe to
do so.
And that's a gift I'll never return.
Love always,
Me
I folded the letter that night.
Slipped it into the back pocket of my journal.
Never mailed it.
But somehow,
it made its way into our life again.
Not in an envelope.
But in the way I started holding you tighter.
In the way I listened more.
In how I started showing up fully, finally.
You never saw the letter.
But I think you felt every word of it
when I chose to stay this time.

Between the Sheets and the Struggles
It used to be easy.
The way our bodies spoke
when our words couldn't.Your breath on my
shoulder.
My hand tracing the shape of your spine.
The comfort of silence between two souls,

that once knew how to hold each other
without needing to explain.
But lately…
The sheets feel colder,
even when we're both under them.
We still touched,
but it wasn't the same.
It wasn't connection
it was habit.
It was ritual
without reverence.
You'd turn off the lamp.
I'd pretend to be asleep.
We were two people
in the same bed
but miles apart.
One night you asked,
"Are we okay?"
And I said, "Yeah."
But I lied.
Because "okay" meant we were coasting.
"Okay" meant we weren't fighting
but also not loving with the same fire.
The truth is,
I missed you
while lying right next to you.
I missed
your curiosity,
your morning laughter,

the way you used to wake me up
just to say "I love you" and fall asleep again.
We tried.We made love out of memory,
not desire.
We kissed with hesitation,
like testing a language we used to be fluent in.
But deep inside
we were still there.
Buried under stress,
deadlines,
expectations,
and the weight of a love that used to feel light.
One morning,
you rolled over and placed your head on my
chest.
No words. Just weight.
And for the first time in weeks,
I didn't flinch.
I placed my hand on your back.
Not for comfort.
But to say,
"I'm still here."
And I felt your breath
slowly syncing with mine.
Your fingers wrapping around my arm.
Not for passion
but for grounding.
Love isn't always loud.
Sometimes it's the quiet act

of choosing to stay in the room.
Of reaching across the silence
and saying:
"Let's start again.
Not from where we left off
but from who we are now."

When Routine Becomes Distance
We didn't notice it at first.
How mornings became mechanicala kiss on
the forehead,
a rushed goodbye,
coffee gone cold in the cup we never finished.
We had a rhythm,
but we lost the melody.
The "How was your day?"
felt more like a checkpoint than curiosity.
We became experts at surviving the day
but amateurs at feeling the night.
We stopped choosing each other
and started assuming each other.
You sat on the left side of the couch.
I scrolled on my phone,
you watched your shows.
We weren't arguing
but that scared me more.
We were becoming roommates
with shared history

but no present.
I remembered when I used to write you
letters
just to say I missed you,
even if you were in the next room.
When I'd surprise you with a playlist,
a note in your lunch,
a forehead kiss in the middle of your rant
just to throw you off and make you smile.
Now I count the times we say "I love you"
as if that proves something.
But the truth is,
even "I love you" started to feel rehearsed.
One Sunday evening,
you stood in the kitchen
still in your oversized hoodie,
your hair messy from a nap you didn't plan.I
looked at you
and something inside me cracked open again.
I walked over,
held your waist,
and whispered:
"I miss us."
You paused,
didn't turn around.
Just leaned back into me.
No words.
Just that lean
like you were saying,

"I miss us too."

Our First Real Fight Since Reuniting
We always knew it would happen.
That one day, the silence wouldn't be soft.
That our calm would crack.
That healing doesn't mean we're immune to
hurt.
It started over something small
a missed call,
a misread tone,
an unfinished sentence turned into
accusation.
But it was never really about that.
It was about everything beneath the surface
the unspoken fears,
the moments we didn't fully forgive,
the parts of us still afraid
we could lose each other again.
You raised your voice.
I folded my arms.
You said, "You're pulling away again."
I said, "You don't see how hard I'm trying."
We stood on opposite ends of the same room,
but it felt like opposite planets.I saw it in your
eyes
not anger, but ache.
You were hurting

because you thought this meant we were failing.
And I was scared too.
Not of the fight itself,
but of what it meant if we couldn't find our way back this time.
Then silence.
Not the good kind.
Not the soft, loving silence we built our love in.
This one was cold.
Sharp.
Walled.
But love real love it doesn't leave when things get hard.
It doesn't slam the door.
It doesn't choose pride over peace.
So I walked over, sat beside you on the edge of the bed,
and said what I never said before:
"I don't need to win.
I just don't want to lose you again."
You looked at me, your eyes glossy with frustration and fatigue.
And you whispered, "I'm just scared... that we'll become them
the people who only survive each other."
I took your hand.
"I'd rather break apart with you and rebuild,

than stay perfect with anyone else."
That night, we cried.
We held each other without trying to fix
everything.
We apologized,
not to be right,
but to be close.And something shifted.
We realized love isn't just the high moments
it's the fight in the middle of the storm.
It's who you choose
when your wounds are showing.
And we chose each other.
Again.

Healing Isn't Linear
They told us healing would take time.
They never said it would take this kind of
time.
The kind that loops you back to places
you thought you'd already left behind.
Some days we're whole
laughing in the kitchen,
dancing in socks on the wooden floor,
sharing meals and soft glances like nothing
ever broke.
Then, without warning, we're back in a silence
that doesn't feel sacred.
I wake up some mornings feeling heavy,

and I can't explain why.
You ask,
"What's wrong?"
And I say,
"Nothing,"
because I don't have the words.
But you know me better now.
You don't push.
You sit close.
You hold space.
That's healing too.
You had a day last week where you shut down
again.Closed the world out.
I saw the fog in your eyes
like you were somewhere else
but sitting right in front of me.
You whispered later,
"I hate that I still get like this."
And I replied,
"I love every version of you,
even the ones that feel like falling apart."
We've both had relapses
into overthinking,
into self-blame,
into trying to carry too much alone.
But every time we do,
we've learned not to run from each other,
but to run to each other.
Healing isn't a staircase.

It's a tide.
Some days it carries you.
Some days it drags you back.
But we promised to swim through it together.
So when your voice shakes,
when my heart goes quiet,
when the world feels too loud
we breathe.
We hold each other in the dark,
and remind ourselves:
This is what love looks like in real time.
Imperfect,
but deeply intentional.
Fragile,
but constantly choosing to stay.

You, Me, and the Future We Weren't Ready
ForThere was a time when love alone felt like
enough.
We made promises with the innocence of
hope
and dreams shaped by midnight
conversations,
headphones shared,
and plans drawn in the air between our
intertwined fingers.
You used to say,
"One day, we'll have a house by the water,"

and I'd smile,
imagining our mornings
coffee, laughter, your robe half falling off your
shoulder.
But life had other plans.
We tried to sprint toward forever
without learning how to walk through the
present.
Bills.
Exhaustion.
Triggers from the past.
My ambition.
Your silence.
And everything in between.
We thought love would be loud enough to
drown it all out.
But sometimes,
love whispers.
And the world is very loud.
I watched you cry in the bathroom once,
thinking I didn't hear.
I stood on the other side of the door,
heart breaking with every muffled sob.
I didn't know how to fix it.
I only knew how to feel it with you.
The truth is:
We wanted a lifetime without learning the
seasons of it.
Spring came easyfresh and full of color.

But we weren't prepared for winter.
We weren't ready for the version of us that
questioned,
that faltered,
that froze over in moments of disconnect.
Still... we survived.
Now when I see you across the room,
shoulders strong but eyes gentle,
I realize something:
The future we weren't ready for
was the one we had to grow into.
Not forced.
Not fantasized.
But earned.
Through hard conversations.
Through sitting with our shadows.
Through loving each other even when the
script fell apart.
We're not chasing the perfect life anymore.
We're building a real one.
Messy. Honest. Full of rewrites.
But ours.
And that's better than anything we ever
imagined.

A Note from the Past
It was buried under old notebooks.
Folded twice, soft at the creases.

Dated two years ago the ink faded but still
readable.
Your handwriting.
My name at the top,as if time hadn't passed,
as if it still mattered.
"If you ever read this, I hope you understand
that silence was never a weapon.
It was a shield.
I loved you in quiet ways because loud love
scared me."
I read those lines over and over.
"Some nights I couldn't sleep because I missed
how we used to talk
with our eyes, with our hands, with our hearts
wide open."
The past has a way of sneaking up on you,
not to haunt, but to remind.
To offer perspective.
To make peace.
This letter didn't feel like reopening a wound
it felt like finding a bandage I didn't know I
needed.
You wrote about how you struggled to
communicate pain.
How your silence was never indifference,
but fear wrapped in pride.
And I realized...
we both had our languages.
Mine was expression.

Yours was restraint.
We just didn't have a translator then.
I folded the letter back slowly.
Not to hide it
but to preserve it.
A relic of who we were.
Proof that even in distance,
you still reached for me
in your own way.Today, I responded in a way
you'll never read:
I whispered thank you into the wind,
and let it carry my forgiveness to wherever
you once sat writing that note.
Because maybe healing isn't only about
closure.
Maybe it's about compassion for the versions
of ourselves
that didn't know better
but still tried.

If Love Could Speak Again
If love could speak again,
it would not shout.
It would not beg.
It would simply whisper:
"I'm still here."
Because love never left.
It just waited.

Waited behind our fears.
Behind our assumptions.
Behind the long silences we used to fill the
void.
I sat across from you at the new place we now
call home.
You were laughing about something on your
phone.
I wasn't listening to the words
I was listening to the moment.
There was a time when I thought I'd never
hear you laugh like that again.
Not with me.
Not in this life.
But love...
it has its way of coming back.
Not always through grand gestures.
Sometimes it's in the way you pour my coffee.
Or how you say "babe" when you're half-
asleep.
Or how we touch feet under the covers and
don't move them away.
If love could speak again,it would tell us that
healing doesn't make us perfect.
It just makes us honest.
That it's okay to be scared again.
Okay to question again.
As long as we keep choosing each other again.
I often ask myself,

what would I say if I had just one chance to
speak to the love we almost lost?
I think I'd say this:
"You didn't fail us.
You just paused.
And in that pause,
we found our rhythm again."
Tonight, as you rest your head on my chest,
I feel your breath match mine
slow, patient, trusting.
And I think:
If love could speak again,
it would sound a lot like this silence.
The kind that finally feels full,
not empty.

Let's Remove Our Doubts, Improve Our Scars
Some days, we didn't speak.
Not out of anger, but weariness.
The kind of silence that settles when you're
both carrying the weight of old
wounds.
We were never trying to hurt each other.
We were just trying to protect ourselves.
But silence, when it's not softened with
love,can cut deeper than words.
One night, you turned to me and asked:
"Do you still doubt us sometimes?"

I didn't lie.
I nodded slowly and said,
"Yes. But I don't let those doubts lead
anymore."
We both have our scars.
Some we gave each other.
Some came long before we ever met.
But now...
we're no longer hiding them.
We're learning to trace them gently,
like love notes written in pain,
reminders that we survived together.
It's easier to show the healed version of
ourselves.
The polished, filtered, put-together parts.
But love doesn't bloom there.
Love grows in the soil of truth.
Messy, real, vulnerable truth.
So we started showing up with our truths.
Even when it was hard.
Even when it hurt.
Even when we had no guarantee the other
would understand.
I remember the night we said:
"Let's stop trying to be perfect.
Let's just be present."
And that was when the shift happened.We no
longer flinch when old memories show up.
We greet them.

Talk about them.
Let them teach us instead of torment us.
We no longer avoid tough conversations.
We sit through them,
even when our voices shake.
And most importantly
we no longer let doubt drive our decisions.
Because even though the road is still long...
we've already chosen to walk it together.
To remove our doubts isn't to pretend we're
unafraid.
It's to believe that love is worth fighting for
again and again.
To improve our scars isn't to erase the past.
It's to allow them to remind us how far we've
come.

The Night He Proposed
We weren't dressed up.
We weren't in a restaurant.
We didn't have a photographer hiding behind
candles and roses.
We were just... us.
You were on the floor with your hoodie
halfway on,
trying to fix the speaker.
I was watching from the couch,

smiling at how you still cursed softly when
you got frustrated.
And then that song came on
"Our song."
The one we made love to the first night we
said, "This is it."
You froze for a moment.
Turned around slowly.
And that's when I knew.
You didn't get down on one knee
immediately.You walked over.
Sat beside me.
reassurance.
Held my hand like you were holding every
version of me that ever needed
Then you whispered:
"We've been through the hardest parts of love.
Now I want to live through the softest parts
with you.
Every ordinary day, every hard moment,
every dance in the kitchen, every storm.
Will you be my wife?"
And even though I already knew my answer,
I cried.
Because it was never about the ring
It was about the promise.
The heart behind it.
The choice.
We danced that night.

Slow.
Offbeat.
Wrapped in each other's arms while the
speaker barely held on to the rhythm.
"Hold me tight 'til the beat goes silent," you
whispered.
And you did.
You held me like you'd never let go again.
That night didn't look like the fairytales.
It was better.
Because it was real.

The Lobola Negotiations
It wasn't just about money.
It never was.
It was about honour.
About showing up for love not just
emotionally, but traditionally.
I remember the nerves in my father's voiceas
he rehearsed what he'd say.
The pride in my uncles as they ironed their
shirts before meeting your family.
And me, pacing the hallway, wondering if this
was still real.
If all the pieces of our broken past had
somehow come together
to build this moment.

Your family welcomed us with firm
handshakes and careful eyes.
Not just to test us,
but to weigh the strength of my intention.
To see if my love was loud enough
to speak their language
the language of respect, heritage, and dignity.
The room filled with gentle silence.
Only the sounds of tradition, laughter, and
negotiation remained.
They spoke of cows,
but really, they were speaking of worth.
They spoke of culture,
but really, they were measuring love.
And I gave all of me that day not just what I
had in my bank account,
but what I had in my heart.
At some point, I caught your mother glancing
at me.
And in her look, I felt two things:
A quiet test... and a quiet blessing.
I passed both.
When the agreement was settled,
your father stood up and said,
"Now we see that this is a man who doesn't
just love our daughter
he's ready to build with her."
I wanted to cry.
But instead, I smiled.

Because this wasn't just a step toward marriage.
It was a step toward becoming a man you and your people could trust.Later that night, I messaged you:
"Today, I didn't just buy cows.
I offered them my love for you.
And they saw it was enough."

What the Cows Couldn't Say
I woke up before the sun did.
My stomach was dancing with nerves.
Not the kind you feel when something is wrong
but the kind you feel when something sacred is about to happen.
This wasn't just another day.
It was the day my family would meet the man I said "yes" to
in heart, in soul, in silence, in everything.
I heard the murmurs from the living room, cups clinking, deep voices humming with both joy and careful respect.
My father was dressed in his finest traditional attire.
My mother wore calm on her face, but I knew better.
She had been praying.

They weren't just negotiating cows.
They were weighing history, value, legacy
and in some ways, the price of the daughter
they had raised
with discipline, pride, and love.
And me?
I sat in my childhood bedroom
reading old journal entries about you.
The first time I called you mine.
The first time you called me "home."
All the quiet nights I dreamt of being yours in
front of our elders,
not just in the hidden corners of our love.
I whispered, "Please don't forget to speak from
your heart."
Even though I knew you would.
When the talks ended and I saw the look on
my father's face,
I knew.
You passed every unspoken test.
Not just because you brought the cows
but because you brought respect.
You brought your people.
You brought your voice and stood like a man
ready to love out loud.
Later, when my mom closed the door to my
room, she said,
"He is yours now. But more than that you are
his."

And I cried.
Not because I was sad.
But because love, when done right,
isn't just loud in words
it's loud in tradition.

The Bachelor Party
It was supposed to be a night of celebration
laughter, drinks, and memories before I said "I
do."
But honestly, I wasn't in it for the wild stories
or crazy dares.
I was in it for the stillness between the noise
a night to reflect with the brothers who knew
me
before love softened my edges.
The boys rented a rooftop spot
city lights glowing, music pulsing,
bottles on the table and secrets in the air.
Some came for the party.I came for the pause.
They toasted to freedom like it was ending.
But I didn't feel like I was losing anything.
I felt like I was stepping into something
sacred.
A promise. A purpose. A peace.
Some laughed about the single days,
while I found myself drifting away
back to the night you fell asleep in my arms,

to the morning you first called me "my love"
with your head buried in my chest.
I wasn't trying to be perfect.
I was just trying to be ready.
One of the guys pulled me aside and asked,
"You sure you want to do this?
You really think forever is a real thing?"
I didn't even blink.
"I've seen forever in her eyes.
I'm not scared of the time
I'm scared of wasting it without her."
They cheered.
They teased.
They danced.
I smiled, but my heart was already home.
Already hearing the music we picked for our
first dance.
Already picturing your dress. Your laugh. Your
love.
I wasn't just preparing for a wedding
I was preparing to become someone's
husband.
Your husband.

The Bachelorette Night I didn't want a wild
night.
No strippers. No crazy games. No loud
confessions.

I just wanted my girls, my laughter, and a little
silence in between
to remind myself who I was before I became
someone's wife.
They booked a beautiful lodge outside the city
fairy lights, champagne, silk robes, music from
the past playing low.
I wore white like a warning:
this heart has loved deeply
and is now preparing to love forever.
There were shots and stories.
Pictures of our childhoods.
Stories of heartbreaks that led us to healing.
In a circle of candlelight, they asked me
"Do you have any regrets?"
And for a second, I felt the weight of
everything I almost lost
the years we didn't speak,
the nights I cried myself to sleep over you,
the doubt that sat between us like fog.
But I looked up and said,
"No. Because every tear taught me to see love
clearer."
I told them how you make me laugh when I
don't feel like it,
how you let me talk when I'm spiraling,
how you hold me with both your body and
your silence.
They clapped when I said I was ready.

Not because I had it all figured out,
but because I was no longer afraid of
staying.Later that night, they left me alone on
the balcony.
City lights blinking in the distance,
stars hanging like soft reminders that the
universe had been listening.
I whispered your name to the wind like a
prayer.
Tomorrow I say yes to you
again, and again, and again

The Night Before the Wedding
I couldn't sleep.
Not from fear, but from gratitude.
The kind that keeps your heart awake even
when your body begs for rest.
I lay there in the guest room at my childhood
home,
the walls still holding echoes of my younger
self
the boy who once wrote songs about
heartbreak,
now writing vows about forever.
My suit was hanging on the door.
Your name, engraved in gold on the inside of
the lapel
Sunflower.

The girl I loved in silence.
The woman I'll soon call my wife.
I thought about texting you.
Just to say I miss you, even in this short space
apart.
But I remembered your rule:
"Let's keep the night before sacred
you and your boys, me and my girls.
Let the silence carry the love."
So I respected it.
Even though my fingers hovered over your
name for a few seconds too long.
There were jokes flying in the house.
Laughter from the bachelor party slowly
fading into night.
My friends were asleep, and I was left with my
thoughts.I sat outside for a while,
cigarette untouched in my hand,
moonlight spilling across the yard like an
open page.
And I wrote:
I don't fear tomorrow, because I've already
found home in you.
I've rehearsed the moment a thousand times
not the walk, not the crowd
just your eyes when they meet mine at the
altar.
No speech could fully hold what I feel for you,
so I'll say it the only way I know how:

through presence, through time,
through forever.
A soft wind passed.
I looked up and whispered to the stars:
"Let her sleep well tonight.
Let her be held in dreams where I'm already
hers."
Tomorrow, I'll see you again.
But not as the girl I once lost.
Not as the friend I once missed.
Not even as the muse who inspired every
page.
Tomorrow, I'll see you as my bride.
And when I say "I do,"
it will echo deeper than a vow
it will be the sound of a life I've been waiting
to begin.

The Night Before the Wedding
I couldn't sleep either.
Not because I was nervous
but because the weight of joy sat gently on my
chest,
like a warm memory refusing to fade.
The girls were asleep, scattered around the
living room,half-finished wine glasses and soft
laughter still hanging in the air.
We had danced, cried, and prayed.

Not just for the wedding,
but for the woman I've become since I first
met you.
My dress hung quietly in the corner.
I stared at it longer than I intended
not because of how beautiful it was,
but because of how much pain, love, healing,
and hope it took to finally stand tall enough to
wear it.
I whispered to it like it could hear me:
Tomorrow... I become your wife.
Not because I need saving,
but because I chose you
again and again, in silence, in storms, in
stillness.
I found an old voice note from you.
It wasn't long, just your voice humming a
melody you said reminded you of me.
I pressed play and let it lull me,
tears slipping out without a warning.
I wasn't crying because I was scared.
I was crying because for the first time in my
life,
I knew what it meant to be truly seen.
I thought about sneaking out to see you.
Even just to hold your hand one last time
before the aisle.
But I held myself back.
This night was sacred.

This silence was sacred.
So I wrote instead:
May you sleep in peace tonight.
May you be wrapped in the arms of your dreams
the ones we once whispered about on broken days.I pray the stars above you hum my name, and the wind reminds you that I've never stopped choosing you.
I crawled into bed with a calm heart.
And before closing my eyes, I whispered:
"God... if I ever doubted love before,
thank You for proving me wrong."
Tomorrow, I wear the dress.
Tomorrow, I say the words.
Tomorrow, I walk toward the one who waited for me
even in silence.

The Wedding
The morning sun broke through the curtains like a quiet blessing.
Soft rays lit the room where I sat, staring at my reflection
not just at the suit, not just at the smile,
but at the man I had become.
Today wasn't just about vows and rings.
It was about survival.

About two souls who once walked away,
but never stopped circling back to each other.
My hands trembled slightly as I adjusted my
cufflinks.
Not out of fear.
But reverence.
Because standing at the altar meant I was no
longer running.
From pain.
From doubt.
From the past.
I waited at the front of the aisle,as everyone
stood.
Then... there she was.
Sunflower.
Floating like a prayer,
wrapped in the dress that held the silence, the
storms, and the survival of our
love.
She wasn't walking toward me
She was returning to me.
And I couldn't breathe.
As her hand slid into mine, time stilled.
Every memory
the midnight drives, the tears, the missed
calls, the healing
gathered in the space between us.
I could hear her heart through her fingers.
The pastor spoke,

but I only remember the look in her eyes
that same look from the first day I knew she
was home.

The Vows
"I loved you in silence before I knew how to
say it aloud.
I choose you now, with a louder heart and
steadier hands.
I promise to grow with you,
to dance with you through life's noise,
and to always come back
even when silence returns."
She spoke next:
"You loved me before you knew my wounds.
You saw the war in my eyes and chose peace
anyway.
I vow to be your rhythm when you lose your
melody.
I vow to build a home within you,
not because you need saving,but because I
want to live in the place your heart calls
home."

We were pronounced husband and wife.
Not just in law, but in soul.
Our first kiss as forever was soft
not because we were shy,

but because we finally understood the
strength it took to make love stay.

The music rose.
The dance floor lit up.
Laughter spilled like wine, and family
wrapped us in warmth.
But even in that noise...
we kept finding each other's hands.
Because after everything
this was the moment our love finally spoke
out loud.

The Wedding
I always imagined what it would feel like
to walk down an aisle not toward a man,
but toward my safest place.
Today, I lived that dream.
The room was quiet when I woke up.
My bridesmaids were still asleep,
but my mind was wide awake
replaying every moment that led to this one.
The heartbreak.
The distance.
The letters unsent.
The day we saw each other again in that
crowded room...
I didn't know then,
that I'd one day walk toward you

with flowers in my handand forever on my
lips.

As they buttoned my dress,
I saw the little girl in me smiling
the one who used to write your name in her
journal,
who imagined a life where love wasn't loud,
but lasting.
My mom cried.
My sister fixed my veil.
And I... I just breathed you in,
from a distance.
I knew you were already there, waiting.
You always waited even when I wasn't ready
to be found.

The doors opened.
Music filled the space.
But your eyes your eyes held me like nothing
else ever could.
You didn't smile like you were impressed.
You smiled like you were grateful.
Like somehow, even after all we've been
through,
you still couldn't believe I chose you.
But I did.
I chose you a thousand times in my silence
before I said it out loud.

When I reached you,
your hands shook.
Mine steadied them.
You whispered, "You're here."
And I whispered back, "I never left."My Vows
to You
You saw me in my darkest season
and still believed in spring.
You loved the broken girl and helped her
rebuild.
I vow to love you when your words are loud,
and when your silence says more than
language can.
I vow to kiss the dreamer and hold the
doubter.
You are my quiet miracle.
You don't just complete me
You remind me I was whole all along.
When they said, "You may now kiss the bride,"
I kissed you like I was saying thank you.
For choosing me when I was hard to love.
For staying.
For growing.
The rest of the night blurred
dances, photos, speeches.
But all I really remember
was your hand on my back,
guiding me gently through the crowd,
as if to say:

"Wherever we go… I'm here."

The Honeymoon
We didn't need paradise.
We just needed peace
and each other.
The sun met us like an old friend that
morning.
You wore linen. I wore nothing but a smile.
The air smelled like ocean salt and second
chances.We weren't running anymore.
Not from pain.
Not from our past.
Not from love.
Just… walking barefoot through new
beginnings.
There was no crowd.
No timeline.
No expectations.
Just two lovers
with tan lines,
slow hands,
and hearts that finally spoke the same rhythm.
We danced under skies that didn't judge.
We kissed without fear of goodbyes.
We held each other like people
who had once been strangers to joy
and were now bathing in it.

I watched you sleep one afternoon,
the way the light kissed your skin
like it knew this body was sacred.
You mumbled my name in a dream.
And I cried not because I was sad,
but because in that moment,
I knew I was home.
We explored beaches like explorers of each
other.
The quiet kind of exploring
Where conversation wasn't necessary,
but connection was constant.
You said:
"I never want to be away from you again."I
replied:
"You don't have to be.
Even when we're apart
I'm with you where it matters most."
We wrote poems in the sand.
Shared secrets in the rain.
Prayed under the stars.
Sang to each other in laughter and silence.
You said this wasn't just a honeymoon.
It was a healing moon.
And maybe that's true.
Because by the time we left,
we weren't just husband and wife.
We were mirrors

reflecting the best and broken in each other,
choosing to stay anyway.
This wasn't just the start of our marriage.
This was the soft rebirth of everything
we had survived to find our way back to.

The Honeymoon
They said the honeymoon would be the
happiest time of our lives
but no one told me how peaceful it would be.
No one told me I'd cry... not from hurt, but
from wholeness.
I watched him laugh by the pool,
dripping wet, messy hair,
pointing out clouds that looked like hearts
and animals.
And I thought to myself:"God, this man is still
the same boy who stole my heart...
but he's grown into a man who now holds it
gently."
The way he looks at me now...
it's not the gaze of someone infatuated.
It's the eyes of someone who has seen me
in chaos, in silence, in doubt
and chose to stay.
That's deeper than love.
That's understanding.
I brought my journal, but I didn't write much.
I didn't need to.

He was everything I used to write about when
I thought I'd never find it.
At night, when he held me...
I felt the echo of every moment I thought I had
lost him.
And now that he was here,
I didn't want to fall asleep
just in case I woke up and it was all a dream.
But it wasn't.
It was us.
Real.
Alive.
Evolving.
We walked the shoreline barefoot.
He let the waves touch his ankles.
I let the wind braid my hair.
We were quiet but it wasn't empty.
It was the silence that comes when love is
safe.I whispered to him one night,
"This is the softest I've ever felt in a world so
hard."
He pulled me closer and said,
"Then let's stay soft even if the world forgets
how."
I don't know what tomorrow holds.
But if it's anything like this...
this sacred calm,
this return to myself,
this choice we keep making every day

Then I want forever.
With him.
In every lifetime.
In every version of us.

The First Morning as Forever
The morning sun crept in slowly,
golden and unhurried,
as if it too understood
the kind of love it was illuminating.
We didn't speak much.
Not because there was nothing to say,
but because everything was already being
said
in the way our hands found each other
beneath the sheets,
in the way his thumb traced circles on my
shoulder,
like he was writing a promise into my skin.
The world outside hadn't changed,
but we had.
We were no longer just two people
trying to get it right.
We were now one home
with two heartbeats.I turned to him, still half-
asleep,
eyes heavy, but spirit weightless.
"Does it feel different?" I asked.

He smiled,
that soft, sleepy smile I'll never forget.
And said,
"No... it feels exactly like you and me.
Just... forever now."
The first breakfast as husband and wife
tasted like ease.
We cooked together
burnt the toast, laughed about it,
danced in pajamas,
kissed with mouths full of jam.
It was unglamorous.
It was unfiltered.
It was ours.
We didn't need fireworks.
Just sunlight, breath, and belonging.
He played our song again.
The one we made love to
the night he proposed.
And in that moment,
we weren't starting something new
we were continuing a sacred rhythm
we had been creating
since the very first "hello."
This was forever.Not because of the wedding,
not because of the rings
but because we chose each other
in every quiet, soft, ordinary morning
like this one.

Return to the World
The wedding was behind us.
But not the meaning.
Not the depth.
Not the intention we carried with us
back into the real world.
Coming home felt like arriving with new eyes.
The same streets,
the same city lights,
the same worn-out coffee shop
but everything looked softer,
because now we were looking together.
We weren't just newlyweds
we were two souls who had endured storms,
who had healed old wounds,
and still chose to stay.
No more rehearsals.
No more "one days."
Just us.
Here.
Now.
Doing the everyday like it was sacred.
Like it was enough.
You see, love isn't proven in the vows.
It's proven in the silence between them.
In how you speak without words.

In how you reach when the other retreats.We
had businesses to build,
dreams to manage,
family expectations to meet.
Life didn't pause just because we fell in love.
But we weren't trying to escape anymore.
We were choosing to build within it.
The little arguments still came.
So did the tired evenings.
The missed calls.
The unread messages.
But this time
there was patience.
There was grace.
We found rhythm in chaos.
We cooked in silence.
We danced in the kitchen.
We worked late and kissed later.
We remembered how to be lovers
while still being partners,
and still being individuals.
Real love is boring sometimes.
But it's the kind of boring
you miss when it's gone.
We came back to a world
that didn't wait for us
but that's okay.
Because we waited for each other.

This wasn't the end of the story.It was just the
end of the chapter
where love had to prove itself.
From here on out,
love just had to live.

"Where Silence Speaks"
We met in the hush
between heartbreak and healing,
when neither of us knew
if love would ever speak again.
But it did.
Not in grand declarations,
not in fireworks or flawless timing
but in gentle returns,
in glances across rooms,
in the space where pain once lived.
You loved me
before I became who I thought I had to be.
You saw me
before I stopped hiding from myself.
And when I crumbled,
you didn't save me
you stayed.
We built our story
on the ruins of what we lost.
No fairytales,
just truth.

No pretending,
just presence.
Now I wake up
to a love that breathes beside me,
not perfect,
but persistent.
Not loud,
but lasting.
We chose this love
with all its silence,with all its noise,
with all its ordinary,
with all its divine.
And I will choose it
again
and again
and again
even when the world forgets how to listen,
even when we forget how to speak.
Because in you,
I found the echo
of everything I thought I lost.
And in us,
silence finally
found its voice.

Chapter 4-*Parenthood, Fame, and Marriage Challenges*

A Year Since 'I Do'
It's been a year since we stood before the world and promised each other forever.
Some days it feels like we said "I do" just yesterday. Other days, like we've been walking this path for decades.
Marriage has a way of humbling you gently and then all at once.
I thought loving her before the vows was the peak. But love after the ceremony?
It's raw. Gritty. Quiet. Real.
It's the mornings she kisses me half-asleep before I leave for work.
It's the way she folds my laundry with intention, even on the days I forget to say thank you.
It's in the silent glances across a room full of people, where her eyes still find mine.
I've grown, in ways no mirror can show.
They say success changes people. Maybe it does.
Business is booming. My name's in rooms I used to pray just to peek into.
But no amount of applause outside will matter if the house I come home to is

silent with tension.
There are days the noise of life drowns the
music of us.
We fight. We forgive. We fight again.
We take breaks mid-argument just to hold
each other not because we're done
talking, but because we refuse to sleep
divided.
I've learned that growth in marriage isn't
about changing the other person.
It's about meeting them, again and again,
through their changes. Through the tired eyes,
through the stretch marks, through the work
stress,
through the parenthood panic, through the
dreams they had before us.
It's been one year.
And if I could, I'd marry her again tomorrow.
Not because it's been perfect but because even
in the chaos, I still find peace in
her arms.
Even when life is loud,
She remains
My silence.

One Year In,
One year.

One year of wearing his last name and waking
up to the same heartbeat that used
to only visit my dreams.
People said the first year of marriage would
be blissful. Others warned it would
be the hardest.
They were both right.
I still remember the way he looked at me at
the altar like the world stood still.
But now, I get to see that look when I'm
wearing a bonnet and a worn-out t-shirt,
sitting on the kitchen floor eating leftovers.
And somehow, that means more.
We've had quiet dinners and loud
misunderstandings.
We've disagreed over tiny things like how to
load the dishwasher and heavier
things like how we both carry stress but show
it differently.
Marriage is a mirror I wasn't ready for.
It shows you where you still need to heal.
Where you still flinch.
Where you still shut down when all they
asked was, "Are you okay?"
Sometimes I find myself missing the simplicity
of dating.
But then he holds me after a long day, when I
don't have words, and I remember:

This version of love the real, unfiltered, early
morning breath, late night tears this
is the kind I prayed for.
He doesn't always get it right. Neither do I.But
we're learning.
To listen without defense.
To love without conditions.
To build without losing ourselves.
There's a version of me that only he sees the
soft one, the undone one, the one
that gets overwhelmed with work, but still
tries to keep us nurtured and
connected.
We've both changed this year.
But the love hasn't weakened it's just grown
stronger roots.
We're not perfect.
But we're planted.
And no storm has made us forget how to
grow.

Fame & Family
There's a strange silence that comes with
success.
I always thought fame would be louder
cameras, interviews, constant attention.
And in some ways, it is.

But behind the flashing lights and carefully crafted captions...
There's still me.
Still the boy who grew up wondering if love and legacy could coexist.
Now I'm a husband, a father-in-the-making, a public figure all at once.
And somehow, the applause doesn't drown out the pressure.
People see us smiling.
They don't see the nights I stay up planning how to keep us grounded.
They don't hear the conversations we have when we're both exhausted but trying
to be present.
They don't know the quiet sacrifices she makes to keep our home feeling like
peace, while I'm out trying to build a life worth coming back to.
Fame taught me that not every eye on you is rooting for you.
But she's been my home in every crowd.
She never cared about the number of followers.
She followed my heart before the world did.
Sometimes, I struggle with being enough for both my purpose and my person.

I want to give her more than just "I'm trying."I
want to give her days where she doesn't have
to wonder if she still matters in
the middle of all this.
She's patient with me.
She listens when my answers don't make
sense yet.
And she reminds me that being known by the
world is nothing if I'm not known
by her.
So even when the world calls,
I return to her voice.
Even when the days stretch me,
I remember the vow we made:
To never lose each other in the noise.

Grief Wears Lipstick
They say grief comes in waves.
But for me, it came in silence.
Not the kind of silence that you sit in to find
peace.
The kind that lingers in the middle of
conversations,
between the clatter of bottles on the dresser,
and the way my voice would crack in the
middle of a sentence I never finished.
The day I lost her my aunt, my second mother,
my first mirror

I wore red lipstick, because that's what she would've wanted.
She always said,
"Don't let the world know you're broken. Let them know you're beautiful."
But I was broken.
Behind every smile was a scream I couldn't let out.
Behind every prayer was a question I didn't dare ask aloud:
Why do the good ones leave so soon?
He held me that night my husband.
He didn't try to fix it.
He didn't say, "She's in a better place."
He just held me,
and in that moment, his silence was the most comforting sound I'd ever heard.
Fame didn't pause for my grief.Work didn't slow down.
Life kept knocking, and I kept answering...
but my heart was slow to catch up.
I've learned grief is not something you get over.
It becomes a room in your heart that you learn to decorate with memories.
And sometimes, when I look in the mirror red lipstick and all
I hear her laugh in mine.
I see her strength in the way I keep going.

She taught me to love with elegance, to lead with softness,
and to never forget where I came from
even when the world forgets who she was.
And so, I wear grief the way she wore her favorite perfume.
Lightly.
With reverence.
With love.

Distance Doesn't Mean Absence
We used to sleep like puzzle pieces.
Curled into each other like we were born for that position.
Now, the bed feels larger.
Not because she's gone but because she's everywhere but here.
Work has taken her to different cities.
Campaigns. Shoots. Features. Appearances.
And me? I'm holding down the fort.
Managing the business, raising our name, shaping our future.
But damn...
Some nights, I don't just miss her I ache for her.
I catch myself staring at old voicemails.
The way she'd say "hey baby" like a love note slipped under the door.
I miss her sarcasm over burnt toast.

Her laugh when I rap offbeat just to make her
laugh harder.
It's not that I don't support her dreams
I do.I always have.
But this kind of distance is unfamiliar.
Different from the one we fought through
three years ago.
Now it's not emotional neglect it's just
logistics.
But even time zones can start to feel like
heartbreak.
We promised each other something real.
Something rooted in purpose.
But purpose doesn't hold you at night.
It doesn't pour coffee in the morning or rub
your back on tired days.
Still, I remind myself:
Distance doesn't mean absence.
It means believing in each other even from
afar.
Loving louder through screens.
Leaving "I miss you" notes under pillows she'll
find days later.
I'm not scared of losing her.
I'm scared she's losing the us that we fought
so hard for.
But I trust her.
And maybe that's what this season is teaching
me

to love her in ways that don't need presence
to be real.
To believe in the silence,
the same way we did at the very beginning.

The Pressure of Being Seen
Every time the camera flashes,
I wonder if they see me...
or the version of me they created.
I'm in hotel rooms more than my own
bedroom.
On flights more than in his arms.
Wearing perfection like makeup
but underneath, I'm just a girl
missing her person.
Fame came with lights, but it also cast
shadows.
Suddenly, I became a symbol.
They call me "inspirational," "gorgeous," "a
goal"
but I'm still learning to be a wife.A future
mother.
A woman balancing passion, pressure, and
presence.
I hear it in his voice when we talk late at night
he misses me.
And I miss him too,
but sometimes I don't know how to say
"I'm tired."

Tired of being strong all the time.
Tired of not knowing how to ask for space
without making it seem like I want distance.
I still keep his voice notes saved.
Replay them in the car,
between interviews and shoots.
They feel like home.
Like warm coffee after a long day.
Like "I got you," even when the world is loud.
I see the doubt in his eyes
when I talk about another opportunity
overseas.
I know he wonders if I'm drifting.
But I'm not.
I'm fighting not just for my dreams
but for our dream too.
He held me through days when I didn't believe
in myself.
Now I want to be a woman he doesn't have to
worry about losing
to the world.
This love
it's not perfect.
But it's real.
And that's what makes me stay grounded.
Even in the pressure,
even when the world is watching,
he still sees me.
The me I sometimes forget to be.

Fame, Faith, and the Fear of Fading
I used to pray for this.The success.
The recognition.
The life I now live.
But no one tells you how loud the silence gets
when you sleep in a big house
without her.
She's out there shining,
like I always knew she would.
Magazine covers, interviews, standing
ovations
and I cheer from the sidelines,
proud... but quietly bruised.
I'm not jealous.
I'm scared.
Scared that the woman I built a life with
might forget the version of me
who sat on the floor with her
sharing noodles and nothing but dreams.
When she walks into the room now,
she's fire and elegance.
But I miss the hoodie, the giggles,
the random kisses in grocery store aisles.
I miss us before everyone knew her.
Sometimes I wonder...
Are we still writing this story together?

Or are we slowly becoming footnotes in each
other's autobiographies?
But then, she turns to me at 2AM
after a show, exhausted,
still whispers,
"I missed you more than the applause."
That's when I remember:
Love doesn't fade.
It just learns to whisper louder
when the world gets noisy.
So I write more music.
I pray harder.
I love her without asking her to slow
downbecause I know she's not running away,
she's just running toward what she always
dreamed of.
And I'm learning to meet her there,
not pull her back.
Faith is loving someone
even when the light is shining so bright on
them
that it makes you squint.
And I still see her.
Even through the glare.
Especially there.

Parenthood in Pause
I hear it every day

"When are you having kids?"
"Don't wait too long."
"Your clock is ticking."
But what they don't see
is the war between my body and my calling.
Between the desire to create life,
and the life I'm still trying to build.
Some nights I cradle my womb with quiet
prayers,
asking it to hold on just a little longer.
Asking it not to see my delay as rejection.
Because it's not that I don't want to be a
mother
I just don't want to lose me while becoming
her.
He never pressures me.
He just listens.
Sometimes he holds me so tightly,
like he's trying to convince my heart
that it doesn't have to choose between dreams
and diapers.
We've had the talks.
The "what if we're not ready?"
The "what if we are?"
And the honest: "what if we never are?"But in
the silence after those conversations,
he always kisses my forehead and says,
"Whenever we do this, it won't be out of fear
or pressure it'll be out of

love."
Still, I wonder if I'm enough right now.
If I'm selfish for waiting.
If I'm broken for not feeling the ache
that others expect me to feel.
But then he looks at me
like I already carry the world in me.
Like I've already mothered poems, projects,
and people.
And he reminds me that timing doesn't
determine love
intention does.
So maybe we'll try next year.
Maybe we won't.
Maybe we'll adopt.
Maybe we'll just keep building
until the walls of our love
are strong enough to raise anything.
Even a child.

Healing While Distant
I never thought we'd be apart this long.
Not emotionally physically.
The miles between us weren't just kilometers,
they were questions we hadn't asked yet.
Fears we were still learning to name.
She got the opportunity of a lifetime.
And I, for the first time in a long time,

had to swallow my pride and say,
"Go. I'll be right here when you return."
It's funny how quiet the apartment feels
without her humming in the kitchen.
Without the sound of her keys hitting the
bowl.
Without her head on my chest,claiming her
usual spot like it was hers before the world
began.
I miss her.
But I don't want to clip her wings
just to keep her close.
That's not love.
So I learned to love her in time zones.
To say goodnight when the sun's still shining
on my side.
To hold my doubts in prayer
and let my faith fill the space where her
presence used to be.
We fought.
Distance exposes the cracks we used to cover
with kisses.
But even in silence, I could feel her trying.
And I was trying too.
Because healing isn't just something we do
side-by-side.
Sometimes, it's done alone,
in airports, in meetings, in unfamiliar hotel
rooms,

while reading the messages she leaves me
before bed.
This is the season we never saw coming.
But it's the one shaping us the most.
And when she comes home
we'll be better, not just together,
but whole within ourselves.

I Didn't Mean to Be Distant
Dear Muse
There were nights I saw you watching me out
loud. I felt your worry, your love, your
confusion.
eyes full of questions you never asked
I wasn't trying to disappear. I was trying to
hold myself together.
Sometimes, I felt like I was drowning in your
tenderness. Not because it wasn't
beautiful but because I didn't know how to
receive it without feeling like I was
taking more than I could give.You looked at
me like I was poetry.
But some days, I didn't even feel like words.

I Loved You Quietly
You loved me out loud with gestures, words,
and presence.
I loved you in the quiet ways:

In the way I memorized your coffee order.
In the way I made space for your thoughts,
even when they tangled.
In how I chose not to leave, even when I was
afraid of staying.
You didn't always notice.
And I didn't always show it right.
But I loved you. God, I did.
Just... differently.

I Felt Like I Was Fading
There was a version of myself I wanted to be
someone whole, present, unshaken.
But each time I tried to meet you in your
depth, I found myself unraveling.
You were fire and I was flicker.
And I didn't know how to tell you that loving
you made me feel more alive and
more lost at the same time.
It wasn't your fault.
You were steady. You were everything.
But I wasn't ready to be seen the way you saw
me.
So I faded.
Quietly.
Painfully.
Out of love not because I didn't feel it, but
because I didn't know how to hold it.

I Heard Every Silence Too
You think I didn't notice the silence growing
between us but I did. I felt it every
time you hesitated before saying "I love you."
Every time your laughter didn't
reach your eyes.You weren't the only one
hurting.
I just got better at pretending I wasn't.
There were days I wanted to reach for you, to
tell you I missed us but by then, it
felt like we were both already halfway out the
door.
Maybe neither of us knew how to stay.
Maybe we both hoped the other would pull us
back.

I Still Think of You
I don't know if I deserve to say this.
But sometimes, I still whisper your name into
the pillow.
Sometimes I find songs you'd love, and I
wonder if you've heard them.
Sometimes, I pass places we went to and I
pause, just for a moment.
You're not just a memory,.
You're a mark.
And no matter how far I've gone,
a part of me still lives in the way you loved
me.

If you ever wonder whether you mattered
You did.
You always will.
Sunflower

Balancing Fame and Foundation
Fame came in quietly,
like a guest who overstays their welcome.
At first, it was flattering
the recognition, the invitations, the
opportunities.
People calling my name in places I'd never
been before.
The light was intoxicating.
But fame has a way of turning people into
glass.
Everyone can see you,
but very few see through you.
She never asked for this spotlight.
Her world was built on moments we kept for
ourselvesprivate laughs, quiet prayers,
unfiltered messiness.
And now, all of it risked being staged for the
world to consume.
I learned quickly that attention can be a thief.
It steals evenings meant for her
and replaces them with flashing lights and
polite conversations.
It demands your presence

while robbing your peace.
Some nights, I'd come home after events
and see her curled up on the couch,
half-watching a show,
half-wondering if this was the life she signed
up for.
It wasn't jealousy
it was the silent ache of sharing someone with
the world.
So I made a promise to her
and to myself.
No matter how bright the lights get,
she will always be my focus.
Our foundation will be stronger than any
stage I stand on.
The applause is temporary.
Her love is not.
Because if I lose her while chasing the world,
then I've already lost everything worth
having.

Balancing Fame and Foundation
When his name started to carry weight,
I felt proud
the kind of pride that makes your chest warm.
I had seen him work for this.
I had prayed for his dreams as if they were my
own.
But I also felt the quiet shift.

Our life began to come with schedules,
calls at odd hours,
dinners that weren't really dinners
but networking in disguise.
I learned to share him
not just with people we knew,but with
strangers who loved him for pieces of him
I used to keep to myself.
I never doubted his love,
but fame has its own language,
and sometimes I didn't know how to translate
it.
I missed the nights where the only thing he
had to be
was mine.
And yet, in the midst of it all,
he never let me fade into the background.
He'd reach for my hand in crowded rooms,
search for me first when the cameras flashed,
lean in and whisper something only meant for
us.
It wasn't always easy,
but I realized
we were learning to grow roots in the middle
of a storm.
The world could have him for a moment,
but I would always have him for a lifetime.

The Weight of Distance
They tell you long-distance is hard.
They don't tell you it's this hard.
We were still married,
still us
but life had stretched us across cities.
My career was calling me to places she
couldn't always follow,
and her own dreams were pulling her in
directions
I wanted her to run toward,
even if it meant away from me for a while.
The phone calls helped.
The late-night video chats helped.
But nothing replaces the warmth of her head
on my chest,
or the way her laughter sounds different in
person
fuller,
like it echoes in my bones.Sometimes I
worried.
Not about her love,
but about the little things distance can steal
inside jokes fading,
routines dissolving,
moments passing without the other there to
witness them.
So I made a promise to myself:
distance would never mean absence.

Every chance I got, I'd show up.
On her good days.
On her bad days.
Even if it was just to hold her for a night
before the morning flight.
Because no matter the miles,
she was still home
and I was determined never to make her feel
like I had left.

Missing You in the Small Things
It wasn't the big moments that hurt the most.
It was the small ones.
Waking up to an empty side of the bed.
Eating breakfast alone.
Laughing at something on TV
and realizing there was no one beside me to
hear it.
We promised each other this distance was
temporary,
a necessary sacrifice for the dreams we were
both chasing.
And I believed that.
But some nights, belief feels paper-thin.
He would call always.
Even if it was just a two-minute check-in
between meetings.
Even if he was exhausted and I could hear it in
his voice.

I knew he was trying,
and I loved him even more for it.
Still, I missed the way his arms could make me
forgetthat the world was too loud,
too fast,
too much.
So I found little ways to keep him here with
me
his hoodie draped over the couch,
our wedding photo by my nightstand,
his cologne sprayed on the pillow before I
slept.
The truth is,
distance doesn't scare me.
What scares me is getting used to it.
And I never want to.

The Weight of the Spotlight
Fame isn't heavy until it starts costing you
time.
I used to think it was just about working hard,
making the right moves,
building something worth being proud of.
But now...
every interview feels like a clock ticking too
loudly.
Every photoshoot steals a weekend.

Every flight means another night she sleeps
alone.
People say I'm living the dream.
And I am.
But what's a dream if the person you want to
share it with
is always on the other side of the phone
screen?
I try to balance it
schedule calls, send voice notes,
make sure she knows that no matter how big
this gets,
she's still the center of it all.
But I can't lie...
there are days I feel like I'm failing her.

I knew what I was signing up for when I
married him.I knew his passion wasn't just a
job
it was part of him.
And I'm proud.
I'm so proud of him it aches sometimes.
But pride doesn't erase the sting of missing
him.
I see his face on billboards before I see it in
person.
I watch interviews where he smiles at the
camera,

but I can tell in his eyes
that he's tired.
That he needs me.
And that I'm too far to reach him.
It's strange
loving someone so deeply,
yet feeling like the world is constantly trying
to share them with you.
I don't want to keep him from his dreams.
I just want to make sure they don't take him
away from ours.

The Distance Between Us
I came home for three days.
Three days.
You'd think that would be enough to hold us
over until the next trip.
But the first night back, we barely talked.
She was quiet, moving around the house like a
ghost.
I tried to lighten the mood
made a joke about how the couch missed me.
She smiled, but it didn't reach her eyes.
By the second day, I couldn't ignore it
anymore.
I asked her what was wrong.
She said, "You're here… but it feels like you're
not."
That one cut deep.

Because I knew she was right.
Even at home, I was checking emails, replying to messages,
trying to keep up with the world outside these walls.
But in doing that, I was letting the world take me away from her.
We didn't argue.We just... sat there,
both of us realizing the same thing
love isn't just about showing up,
it's about being present.

I'd been counting down the days until he came home.
Three weeks of phone calls,
three weeks of missing the way he feels when he hugs me,
three weeks of falling asleep alone.
But when he finally walked through the door,
it didn't feel like the movies.
It didn't feel like the warmth rushing back into the room.
It felt... distant.
Like his body was here, but his mind was still in a meeting somewhere else.
I didn't want to ruin the little time we had by nagging.
So I kept quiet.

But silence can be heavy,
and by the second day, he asked.
And when I told him how I felt,
I watched the guilt cross his face.
We didn't fight.
We didn't raise our voices.
We just let the truth sit between us like an open wound.
And in that moment, I realized
if we didn't guard this marriage from the noise of the world,
the world would gladly take it from us.

The Promise We Made
The morning before I left again,
I woke up early and just... watched her sleep.
The way her hand rested near her face,
how her hair spilled across the pillow like it belonged there forever.I thought about what she said "You're here... but it feels like you're not."
And I realized, if I didn't fix this now,
we'd start to feel like strangers in our own home.
So over breakfast, I told her:
"From now on, when I'm home, the world can wait."
No emails.
No calls unless it's family.

No social media scrolling while we're
together.
She raised her eyebrow, skeptical.
"You think you can actually do that?" she
asked.
I smiled.
"For you? I'll try harder than I've tried for
anything."
We shook on it.
Like kids making a pact.
But this wasn't just a promise it was our
lifeline.

When he said it, I almost didn't believe him.
Not because I thought he couldn't keep his
word,
but because I knew how the world tugs at him.
But then he reached across the table,
took my hand,
and for a second, I saw the man I fell in love
with in the quiet beginnings.
I didn't need big speeches.
I just needed his presence.
His full attention,
like I was the only thing that mattered in the
moment.
We decided on "sacred hours"
from dinner until bedtime,
no work, no calls, no distractions.

Just us.
It felt simple.
Almost too simple.But as we sat there
finishing our coffee,
I realized love survives in the small,
intentional things.
And maybe, just maybe,
this promise could save us from the slow drift
apart.

Sacred Hours Tested
It was only three days after we made the
promise when the test came.
I was halfway through making dinner with her
chicken sizzling, wine glasses half
full
when my phone lit up on the counter.
The name flashing on the screen wasn't one I
could easily ignore.
A big client.
One of those calls that could open doors you
dream of your whole career.
I froze.
The sound of the phone ringing suddenly felt
louder than the pan,
louder than the music playing softly in the
background.
She glanced at the phone.
Then at me.

No words just that raised eyebrow again.
I thought about all the reasons I should
answer.
All the ways I could justify breaking the rule
just this once.
But then I looked at her.
The candlelight dancing in her eyes.
The way she was trying not to look
disappointed, like she was bracing for me to
choose work over us again.
I reached over,
flipped the phone face-down,
and turned back to stir the chicken.
Her smile came slow,
but when it did, it was worth more than any
deal.

The phone rang and I swear my heart sank.
Not because I didn't understand his world
I did.
But because I knew how often it swallowed
him whole.
I waited for the familiar pattern:
Him muttering, "Just one second,"
walking away,
and me finishing dinner alone.
But he didn't.
He didn't even touch the phone except to hide
it.

Like it wasn't even an option.
I tried to play it cool,
but inside, something shifted.
It wasn't about the phone.
It was about the fact that he remembered
remembered that this hour was ours,
and chose to keep it that way.
We ate dinner with no interruptions.
No screens.
Just the sound of forks on plates,
and that easy laughter we hadn't shared in
weeks.
That night, I fell asleep thinking
maybe promises can survive if they're
protected in the smallest moments.

The Temptation on Her Side
It happened on a Thursday.
He was out at the studio, and I had the
apartment to myself.
The kind of quiet that makes you hear every
creak of the walls.
I'd been feeling... restless.
The baby was finally down for a nap,
and I'd been scrolling through my messages
when I saw it,
a text from an old friend I hadn't heard from
in years.

He was in town.Said he missed the way I used
to light up a room.
The kind of message that flattered more than
it should have.
I stared at it, my heart pounding in my ears.
It wasn't about wanting him
it was about wanting a piece of myself I hadn't
seen in a long time.
The carefree version of me, before diapers,
deadlines, and the constant stretch
between wife, mother, and woman.
The "what if" part of my mind whispered: It's
just a coffee.
The "we promised" part reminded me: Sacred
hours aren't just for dinner they're
for protecting us.
I deleted the message.
Then I put my phone face-down,
just like he did that night with the client call.

When I got home, she was quieter than usual.
Not the kind of quiet that meant she was upset
the kind that meant she was holding
something.
We curled up on the couch,
her head on my chest,
and after a while she whispered,
"I almost broke it today."
She told me everything.

Not in a defensive way.
Not with shame.
Just... honest.
And in that moment,
I realized that our promise wasn't about never
being tempted.
It was about trusting each other enough to
admit when we were.
I kissed her hair and said,
"Thank you for choosing us. Again."
She smiled small, tired, but real.
And I held her a little tighter,because
sometimes the smallest confessions feel like
the loudest declarations of
love.

When the World Wants More of Us Than We
Can Give
It started with the phone ringing nonstop.
Our faces were everywhere magazine covers,
interviews, trending tags.
The album had blown up in ways I never
imagined.
Every manager, sponsor, and journalist
wanted "just fifteen minutes."
Fifteen minutes here, fifteen there...
until there was nothing left for us.
One night, I got a call from a late-night talk
show host's producer.

It was the kind of slot that could open even
bigger doors.
The problem?
It was during our sacred hours.
I stared at the phone, thumb hovering over
"accept."
This wasn't temptation from another person
it was temptation from the dream I'd been
chasing for years.
A dream I wanted her and our child to benefit
from.
But then I remembered
if I broke the promise for my dream,
I might wake up one day without the thing
that mattered more than any stage.
I told them I couldn't do it.
They didn't understand.
But she would.

I could hear the phone vibrating from the
kitchen.
He didn't tell me about the call right away,
but I saw it in his eyes when he walked in
that look people get when they've turned
something down they secretly wanted.
He just sat down next to me,
took my hand,
and said, "I chose us."

I didn't ask what he turned down.
Because I knew that if it mattered enough to him to mention it,
it was something big.
Bigger than me, even.
But in that moment, I realized
love is made up of invisible sacrifices.
Ones the world will never applaud you for.
Ones that don't trend,
but keep your home warm.
And I silently promised to keep making mine too,
even if no one saw them.

When Promises Bloom
They hadn't expected the quiet morning to feel like a celebration.
Sunlight spilled through the curtains,
warming the bed they shared.
He reached for her hand first
a small, familiar gesture that felt like home.
She smiled,
eyes still heavy with sleep but shining with something new.
Their baby cooed softly in the crib nearby,
the sound weaving through the quiet like a melody.
They had fought for this
the sacred hours, the long-distance nights,

the moments where the world tried to pull
them apart.
But here they were.
Stronger.
Together.
A family.
He whispered,
"We made it."She nodded,
"Because we chose each other. Every day."
No flashbulbs.
No cameras.
Just love.
Raw, imperfect, and real.
And in that moment,
everything they had promised
bloomed
quietly, fiercely, beautifully.

"In the Quiet Between Us"
In the quiet between us,
where words fall soft and slow,
love speaks louder than noise,
and hearts learn how to grow.
Through miles stretched like shadows,
and nights filled with doubt,
we held onto whispers,
the promises we vowed.
Fame tried to steal our moments,

and distance dared to divide,
but in sacred hours chosen,
we found our truth inside.
Not perfect, not easy,
but honest and true
love is the space we make,
between me and you.
So here's to the battles,
the laughter, the tears,
to choosing each other
through all of the years.
For love isn't silence
it's the music we play,
in the quiet between us,
where forever will stay.

Chapter 5-*Three Years Later: Reunion and Reflection*

When the World Feels Closer
One More Morning Together,
The smell of freshly brewed coffee drifts
through the kitchen as sunlight spills
lazily through the blinds.

The children's voices carry from the living
room giggles, small feet tapping on
the wooden floor.
She sits across from me, hair still messy from
sleep, wearing the oversized shirt I
gave her years ago.
We don't talk much this morning; sometimes
silence says more than
conversation ever could.
It's a fragile kind of peace, the kind that makes
you want to freeze time.
In the back of my mind, I know the phone will
ring soon a reminder that the
world out there is waiting to pull me away.

Whispers Through the Walls
The walls in our home are thin.
They weren't built for secrets.
We didn't know they were listening the little
ears in the hallway.
It wasn't an argument, just two adults trying
to navigate something that doesn't
have a rulebook:
how to raise children while living in the public
eye.But when I caught my daughter's wide-
eyed gaze from the doorway,
I realized the cost of every whispered
disagreement isn't just ours to pay.

The Interview
They promised it would be light-hearted "fun
questions, nothing too personal."
But the second the cameras started rolling, I
felt the familiar shift.
They asked about us. About the kids. About
the rumours.
She smiled through it, polished and poised,
but her hand found mine under the table,
gripping tighter each time the conversation
strayed too close to home.
We left the studio smiling for the paparazzi,
but the ride home was nothing but quiet roads
and thoughts we weren't ready to
share.

Fame's Unwanted Gift
It started small a stranger at the supermarket
calling the kids by name.
Then came the photos online, the fan pages,
the commentary on how they looked, what
they wore, what kind of parents we
must be.
The line between admiration and intrusion is
paper-thin.

And now, even home feels like glass
transparent, fragile, one crack away from
shattering.

A Quiet Argument
It's not shouting. It's the kind of argument that
simmers low and burns slow.
Her voice stays soft, but the weight in her
words is heavy.
We sit at opposite ends of the couch,
debating whether to share less with the public
or trust that the world will be
kind.
The truth is, I don't know which answer is
right.
And she's starting to believe I'm choosing
ambition over peace.

The Fragile Balance
A Mother's Shield, the world doesn't see the
way I hover in doorways, listening for the
sound of my
children's laughter,
checking that their joy is untouched.
They don't see how I mute the television when
news about us plays,
or how I scroll past articles with my own face
on them

not because I'm afraid of what they'll say about me,
but because I'm afraid of what they might one day say about my children.
Protecting them has become more than a choice. It's instinct. It's my heartbeat.

Between the Dream and the Duty
I worked years for this the career, the recognition, the open doors.
But nobody tells you that success comes with its own kind of loneliness.
Some nights, I stare at the ceiling wondering if I've built a life I can't fully live in.
I want to provide for them, give them more than I had
but I also want to be here to watch them grow.
The dream and the duty… they're pulling me in opposite directions,
and my arms are starting to ache from holding both.

When Love Feels Stretched
It's in the way our conversations shrink.
They used to be rivers, flowing for hours.
Now they're puddles, shallow and scattered.
We speak in to-do lists and schedules,

forgetting the poetry of small talk, the soft in-
between moments that used to bind
us.
We still love each other but sometimes it feels
like we're loving from a distance,
even when we're sitting side by side.

The Unopened Letter
It came in a plain envelope,
the handwriting on the front pulling me back
years in an instant.
I didn't open it.
Not because I didn't want to know what it
said,
but because I already knew that whatever was
inside
would stir something I wasn't ready to feel.
I slid it into the drawer by my bedside,telling
myself I'd read it one day
but maybe I'm just waiting for the day it no
longer matters.

Storm at the Dinner Table
The children were telling us about their day.
Then something small something ridiculous
turned into a full-blown argument between
us.
Not yelling, but sharp enough for the kids to
notice.

They went quiet, their forks pushing food in slow circles.
In that moment, I hated myself for letting our tension spill over into their space.
We spent the rest of the night pretending everything was fine,
but the air in the house carried the storm long after we stopped speaking.

Breaking and Mending
The Day She Left for a Week,
It wasn't a fight that drove her out not exactly.
It was accumulation.
Too many late nights apart.
Too many conversations cut short by phone calls.
Too many moments where I thought "later" would be enough.
She packed light. Just a small suitcase and a sweater I'd seen her wear on our first trip together.
She didn't slam the door.
The silence it left behind was loud enough.

Breathing Without Him
The air felt different in the guest room at my sister's place.
No cameras, no questions, no eyes watching us through the glass of our own

lives.
I could hear myself think again.
It scared me how easily I fell back into the rhythm of being alone.
But I missed him not the version of him the world got to see,
but the one who used to leave handwritten notes in my bag,
the one who laughed like the whole world had just let him in on a secret.
I wondered if he missed me too... or if he just missed the idea of me.

Empty Mornings
The first morning without her felt like a mistake I couldn't undo.
I kept pouring two cups of coffee out of habit, forgetting she wasn't there to take the second one.
The kids noticed the quiet.
I told them Mom was taking some time for herself
but the truth was, I needed her here more than I was ready to admit.
At night, I wrote her letters I never sent.
Maybe because I didn't know how to ask her to come home
without admitting I was the reason she left.

The Unexpected Call
It came just after midnight.
Her voice was shaking,
but before she could say it, I already knew
something was wrong.
A family emergency.
All the petty arguments, all the stubborn
silences
they vanished the second I heard the words.
I told her I'd be there in twenty minutes.
Distance doesn't matter when the heart
decides it's already home.

By the Hospital Bed
The room was too bright, too clean,
too full of beeping machines that sounded like
reminders of how fragile
everything is.
We stood side by side, holding onto each other
like the world could disappear if
we let go.
In that moment, I wasn't a husband defending
his pride,
and she wasn't a wife building her walls.
We were just two people who loved the same
people too much to waste time on
being right.

Somewhere in that sterile, white room,
we remembered how to love each other
without needing to win.

Between Us and the World A Promise in the
Dark
We were lying in bed, lights off, the city
humming faintly outside the window.
I couldn't see her face, but I could feel her
breathing slow, steady, warmer than
the blanket we shared.
I told her I didn't want to lose us again.
She didn't answer right away.
When she finally spoke, her voice was soft,
like the sound of someone placing a fragile
object back where it belongs.
"We keep the world out," she said, "and let
each other in."
That was the promise not just to stay, but to
protect the space we call us.

Teaching the Children About Love
It wasn't a lecture.
It was pancakes on a Saturday morning,
a conversation about kindness and
forgiveness between sips of orange juice.
They're too young to understand marriage,
but they know when a home feels heavy.

We told them love isn't about never fighting
it's about finding each other again
after you do.
And as they nodded, syrup on their cheeks,
I prayed they'd remember that lesson longer
than they remember the times we
failed to live it.

Loving Him Louder
I used to keep certain parts of my love quiet
the compliments in my head, the gratitude I
felt but never voiced.
But after almost losing us, I decided to love
him like someone might take him
away tomorrow.
I tell him when I notice the little things.
I touch him when I pass by,
not because I have to, but because I get to.
And maybe that's what keeps love alive
not just holding on in the storms,
but holding on tighter when the skies are
clear.

Guarding Our HomeI started saying "no"
more.
Not to her, not to the kids to the world.
No to interviews that wanted to pry.
No to appearances that took me away for no
good reason.

No to letting strangers have a say in the way
we live.
Our home is not for public consumption.
It's a place for laughter, for arguments that
end with hugs,
for love that doesn't need to be posted to be
real.

The World Outside the Window
One evening, we stood at the window,
the city lights stretching out beneath us like
an ocean of possibilities.
The world will always be there bright,
tempting, loud.
But in that moment, we realized something
simple:
we don't owe it all of us.
We owe ourselves to each other.
And as the reflection of our family filled the
glass,
I knew the world could wait.

A Year Later
The seasons turned quietly.
The kids grew taller, their laughter carrying
further down the hallway.
We still argued sometimes about dishes, about
schedules, about nothing at all

but the difference now was that the
arguments ended with arms around each
other,
not backs turned in bed.
The world was still loud, still knocking at our
door,
but we'd learned to let it wait on the porch.

Their Words
One evening, as I tucked our daughter into
bed,
she looked at me and said,
"I like it when you and Mom smile at each
other. The house feels warmer."
It was a simple sentence,but it hit like a truth I
should have never forgotten:
our love doesn't just belong to us
it shapes the world our children live in.

The Shape of Peace
I used to think peace meant quiet.
Now I know it's not about the absence of noise
it's about knowing which sounds matter.
The laughter in the kitchen.
The patter of little feet in the morning.
The way his voice softens when he says my
name.

Peace is the choice to hold onto these things
and let the rest fade away.

The Longest Promise
We've been through storms,
through days where the air between us felt
cold,
and nights where I thought love alone might
not be enough.
But here we are not perfect, not without scars
just steady.
And maybe that's what marriage really is:
not a fairytale without flaws,
but the longest promise you keep making,
even when it's hard.

Echoes of What Was
On quiet nights, I still think about the times
we almost lost this.
Not to dwell
but to remember that love is not guaranteed.
It's a garden we keep tending,
a house we keep building,
a song we keep singing together,
even when the melody changes.
And as I lay beside her, the world outside our
window fading into the

background,
I realize the truth I've always known:
silence isn't empty when it's filled with love.

"To the days we almost gave up,
and the nights we chose to stay.
To the hands that learned
how to hold each other again,
even when they had grown cold.
To the laughter we guarded,
the tears we didn't hide,
and the walls we kept strong enough
to keep the world out
but soft enough to let love in.
May we never forget
that silence is not the absence of words,
but the space where hearts
can hear each other clearly.
And may the world outside
never matter more
than the one we've built here,
between us."

Chapter 6-*Continuing Journey of Healing and Emotional Reflection*

Dawn of Change

The world was quiet, but my mind was not. The echoes of yesterday's choices still lingered, heavy and restless, like rainclouds unwilling to break. I sat by the window, tracing the faint lines of light creeping across the floor, wondering if sunlight could ever feel as warm again.

Her laughter, so vivid in memory, haunted the edges of my thoughts. I wanted to call her name, but words seemed too fragile, too human, to capture the weight of everything unsaid. I realized then that silence wasn't emptiness it was a space where love lingered, waiting for courage to return.

I closed my eyes and let the memories wash over me: the late-night drives, her hand finding mine without asking, the way her presence could quiet storms inside me. The future felt uncertain, but something in that uncertainty whispered possibility. Maybe healing wasn't a destination it was a choice, moment by moment, breath by breath.

Morning came slowly, spilling soft gold across the walls. I stayed still, listening to the rhythm of the house, to the faint hum of a city waking up. I felt him before I saw him like gravity pulling, inevitable and constant.

Yesterday's pain was still a shadow, but it felt less like a weight and more like a reminder. A reminder that love could hurt, but it could also endure. I traced my fingers along the windowpane, imagining the paths we had yet to walk together.

I thought of the letters we never sent, the words we swallowed in silence, and I realized that maybe this quiet was a chance to speak truth without fear. Maybe this dawn was not an ending it was a beginning, fragile and uncertain, but ours.

We did not speak. The room held a shared understanding, a fragile truce between hearts still raw but willing. Outside, the city stretched, indifferent and alive. Inside, our hearts stirred with a new rhythm a rhythm of cautious hope, quiet strength, and love still learning to breathe again.

The dawn was more than light. It was a chance. And for the first time in a long time, we believed in the possibility of everything to come.

Quiet Conversations

I found her in the kitchen, the morning light catching the soft waves of her hair. She didn't notice me at first, lost in the ritual of making coffee, as if the world outside could wait. I lingered in the doorway, watching the subtle movements that had always mesmerized me the way her fingers paused mid-air, the way her eyes traced invisible patterns on the counter.

"Good morning," I said softly, and she startled, a gentle smile spreading across her face. It was small, but it felt like a victory.

We sat at the table, not touching yet, but close enough that our elbows brushed, sending sparks through the quiet. Words came slowly, cautiously, each one measured.

"I... I've been thinking," I began, "about us. About what we've been through, and what we're still willing to fight for."

She didn't answer immediately. She never did when her mind was weaving through emotions too vast for speech. I let silence fill the spaces between us, learning again how weightless and heavy it could be at the same time.

I watched him struggle with the words he needed to say, his vulnerability shining brighter than any declaration of love could. There was something sacred in this moment the slow unwrapping of ourselves, piece by fragile piece.

"I've been scared," I admitted, my voice barely above a whisper. "Scared that we couldn't survive everything... scared that I might lose myself along the way."

He reached across the table, finally bridging the distance, his hand finding mine. The touch was not urgent, not demanding simply present, grounding.

"I'm here," he said. "And I'm not going anywhere. We'll figure it out, together. Even if it's messy, even if it hurts, even if it scares us. We'll find our way."

And in that quiet exchange, I realized that love wasn't only in grand gestures or perfect moments it was in the willingness to stay, to listen, to be present. To speak and to hear, and to sit with each other when words failed.

The morning lingered like a soft song, its notes carried on the gentle warmth of sunlight. We didn't need more than this to be close, to share a space, to acknowledge the fragility and strength entwined within us.

It was a conversation without words at times, a language of glances, breaths, and the unspoken promise that no matter the storms outside, we were still learning the art of standing together.

And in that quiet, I felt it hope, tentative and tender, growing into something stronger with each heartbeat.

Echoes of the Past
The quiet moments carried ghosts. I felt them in the spaces between our words, in the shadows cast by the morning sun. Memories surfaced unbidden sharp and tender all at once. I remembered arguments I never wanted to have, moments of pride and stubbornness, the times I let fear guide me instead of love.

I caught a glimpse of her from across the room, her silhouette outlined by the window. She moved with the same grace, the same determination, yet there was a fragility I hadn't noticed before. A reminder that she too carried echoes of pain old wounds that had never fully healed.

I wanted to reach across time and undo everything that had hurt her, but the past had already been written. All I could do now was offer presence, understanding, and a steady hand to hold.

I saw him staring out the window, lost in thought, and I knew he was remembering too. I could feel the weight of all the unsaid apologies, all the moments when love had faltered under the pressure of life.

My own memories twisted in my chest: the nights I cried alone, the times I doubted myself, the fleeting sense that maybe we weren't enough for each other. And yet, sitting there in the soft morning light, I realized that even those memories were a part of us shaping, molding, teaching us how to hold on.

"Do you ever wish things could be different?" I asked, breaking the quiet.

He turned to me, eyes shadowed but honest. "I do," he admitted. "But then I think... maybe we need all of it the mistakes, the pain, the echoes. Maybe they brought us here, to this exact moment."

And in that admission, I found a strange comfort. That our past, no matter how heavy, had carved a path toward something deeper, something worth protecting.

We didn't rush to fill the room with words after that. Instead, we let the echoes settle around us, letting the ghosts coexist with the present. Each memory, each shadow, became a thread in the tapestry of what we were rebuilding.

In that quiet, I felt the fragile strength of trust returning, the gentle courage to face the past without fear. And I knew, in the softest corner of my heart, that love wasn't just surviving it was learning, evolving, and daring to hope again.

Career Crossroads

The offer arrived in the quiet of an ordinary afternoon, an email glowing on the screen like a doorway to another life. A prestigious opportunity, far away, demanding more than I could imagine more than either of us could anticipate. My heart leapt, but then hesitated. Excitement tangled with fear, ambition clashing with loyalty.

I looked across the room at her, engrossed in her own work, the sunlight catching the edges of her notebook. How could I chase a dream that might pull me from her? And yet... what if not pursuing it meant betraying myself?

I wrestled with words I hadn't yet formed. I wanted her to understand without judgment, to see that this wasn't a choice against her, but a step toward becoming more together and apart, if we could manage the distance.

I noticed his tension before he even spoke, the way his hand hovered over the laptop keyboard, the slight furrow of his brow. I knew that look ambition mixed with fear, desire mixed with doubt.

When he finally spoke, I listened with all of me. "They want me... far away," he said. "It's everything I've worked for, but I don't want to leave us behind."

My chest tightened. Pride and worry collided inside me. I wanted him to soar, to claim what he'd earned, but I also feared the distance, the quiet nights without the warmth of his presence.

"Then we'll figure it out," I whispered, reaching for his hand. "If it's right, it will survive. And if it's hard, we'll survive harder. We've already faced storms we can navigate this too."

We sat there, fingers intertwined, letting the weight of the decision rest gently on both of us. No promises were made, no solutions offered yet. Just the quiet understanding that life demanded choices, and love demanded courage to face them together.

In that fragile balance of ambition and devotion, I realized that love wasn't about holding each other in place it was about holding each other steady, no matter where life's currents carried us. And somehow, in the silence of that room, we found the courage to imagine the future uncertain, challenging, but ours to shape.

Testing Trust
The first tension came quietly, almost unnoticed, like a shadow slipping across sunlight. A friend called, casually dropping details about a project details I hadn't shared with her yet. I could see her reaction before it even fully formed: the crease between her brows, the pause in her breath.

I hated that I had allowed space for doubt. I had thought we were unshakable, that our trust was solid and unbreakable. But life, it seemed, was patient in testing even the strongest foundations.

I wanted to explain, to bridge the gap with words that carried truth and intention, but I hesitated. Words, I realized, could sometimes falter where presence and sincerity mattered most.

I felt it immediately the flicker of uncertainty, a small quake beneath the surface. His silence, the half-truths of timing, the space between what he said and what I sensed it pricked at me, sharp and insistent.

I wanted to confront, to demand clarity, but I paused. I remembered how far we had come, how fragile our reconciliation still was. Trust, I realized, wasn't a single act it was a daily decision, a rhythm we had to honor even when it trembled.

"Are we... okay?" I asked softly, testing the air, willing him to meet my gaze.

His eyes softened, weighted with remorse and honesty. "We are," he said. "But I see now how easily even small shadows can creep in. I'll be more careful, more present. Always."

The afternoon stretched, a quiet testament to the delicate balance between love and doubt. We spoke little, but each glance, each touch, carried reassurance heavier than words.

It was a reminder that love, even after storms, was not invincible but it was worth tending. Worth staying, worth rebuilding, worth trusting again.

And in that quiet room, with sunlight filtering through the blinds, we chose to believe not in perfection, but in the strength of our commitment.

Hidden Letters/Secrets
I found it tucked behind the stack of books on the shelf a letter I hadn't seen before, folded carefully, edges worn like it had waited years to be discovered. My pulse quickened as I opened it, hesitating over the delicate handwriting that spoke of truths I hadn't known, and fears she hadn't voiced.

Her words were raw, unguarded, and brimming with memories I hadn't been part of. I felt a pang of guilt and awe guilt for the distance that had allowed silence to grow, and awe for her courage to write the words she might never have spoken aloud.

I realized then that love carried layers we could never fully see. Each secret, each hidden thought, was part of the map of her heart. And the question wasn't whether I could forgive the unseen it was whether I could hold her trust, now that the truth had revealed itself.

I noticed him reading it before I could stop him, my heart thumping in sudden panic. I had written that letter in the early days of uncertainty, when words were safer than conversations. I had hoped it would never be needed but perhaps some truths are meant to surface when timing finally allows.

He looked up at me, eyes wide with understanding and something deeper a reverence for the fragility of what I had written, and the strength it had taken to write it.

"I... I didn't know," he said softly. "I wish I had, sooner. But I see now. I see all of it."

I nodded, voice barely a whisper. "It was never about hiding. It was about being ready... about trusting you enough to finally let you in."

We sat there, the letter resting between us, a bridge of vulnerability and honesty. The room felt heavier, yet lighter, as though the truth had filled the spaces silence had left.

It was a reminder that secrets were not always betrayals they were sometimes protective shields, waiting for the right moment to dissolve. And in that quiet, fragile space, we found something rare: the courage to hold each other without fear, to step closer even when the past threatened to linger.

The dawn of understanding was slow, but real. And in that understanding, we glimpsed the resilience of love the quiet strength that grows not in perfection, but in the courage to reveal and to receive, without judgment.

Small Joys, Big Love

It was in the quiet, ordinary moments that I found her most captivating. The way she hummed softly while cooking, the gentle tilt of her head as she read aloud a line from a book, the way her laughter lingered long after the sound faded.

I realized that love was not always the grand gestures or dramatic declarations it was in the small, unassuming moments that stitched our hearts closer together. A shared cup of tea in the morning, a brush of fingers in passing, a look that said, *I see you. I choose you.*

For the first time in weeks, I felt unburdened, not because the past had disappeared, but because I understood that the present held its own kind of magic. Each smile, each touch, was a thread weaving us back into one another's lives.

I watched him across the room, noticing the subtle changes the ease in his posture, the softness in his eyes, the way he lingered in my presence without expectation. It was comforting, grounding, and oddly exhilarating all at once.

We danced around each other in our routines, laughing at small mishaps, stealing glances over steaming mugs of coffee, sharing fleeting touches that spoke louder than words. It was a gentle rediscovery of intimacy, a reminder that love thrives not only in extraordinary moments but in the quiet accumulation of everyday joys.

And in those moments, I realized: we were building something resilient. Something that could weather storms, survive silence, and blossom in the tender spaces between hearts.

The evening light spilled across the floor, warm and golden, and we lingered there without speaking, letting presence replace words. It was a quiet celebration of us a love renewed in subtle, profound ways.

We understood, silently, that happiness wasn't always dramatic or loud. Sometimes, it was found in the ordinary, the shared, the unspoken. And in that understanding, we discovered the simple truth: love, when nurtured patiently and tenderly, could be infinitely larger than any fear, any doubt, any past hurt.

Journey Together

The airport was bustling, alive with the hum of movement and possibility. I watched her navigate the crowd with quiet confidence, suitcase in hand, and felt a surge of pride mixed with a strange ache I was about to leave the familiar cocoon of home, yet I was doing it with her by my side.

Travel had always been a metaphor for us: movement, discovery, the unknown. But now it was tangible, real. Every glance we shared in the fleeting chaos of departures and arrivals was a reminder that we were not just journeying through places, but through life together.

I caught her hand as we navigated the terminal, our fingers entwining naturally, as if they had always belonged there. The world around us blurred, motion and noise fading into insignificance. In that moment, I realized that wherever we went, as long as we were together, we were home.

The plane lifted off the ground with a roar and a sudden freedom that made my chest tighten not from fear, but from exhilaration. I watched the city shrink beneath us, the streets and rooftops becoming lines and shapes, and I thought about the life we were carrying with us: fragile, beautiful, and uncharted.

He turned to me with a soft smile, the kind that made my heart clench in recognition of all the quiet ways he loved me. "Are you ready?" he asked, not for the trip, but for the journey we were on together, for the challenges and revelations yet to come.

I nodded, squeezing his hand. "As ready as we'll ever be. Let's see where this takes us together."

The days that followed were a montage of quiet discoveries: early morning walks along foreign streets, laughter echoing across unfamiliar cafes, the sensation of new air filling our lungs and hearts alike.

We photographed nothing, not for memory or validation, but for the sheer joy of noticing to catch the flicker of sunlight on her hair, the curve of his smile in reflection, the way the world seemed to slow when we were present with each other.

And in those shared moments, I realized that a journey was never just about the destination. It was about the companionship, the unspoken understanding, the subtle exchanges that deepened love and trust in ways words could never fully capture.

The world was vast, unpredictable, and sometimes terrifying but with him beside me, every step felt certain, every horizon inviting.

Crisis & Choice

The call came unexpectedly, sharp and urgent, like a storm breaking over calm waters. Family troubles, complicated and layered, demanded immediate attention. My heart raced, not just from the weight of the news, but from the knowledge that this would test us in ways we hadn't yet faced.

I looked at her across the room, feeling the tension coil between us. How could I protect her from the chaos? How could I balance duty, ambition, and love without losing something essential?

"I have to go," I said quietly, the words heavy with unspoken fear. "But I need you with me, in thought, in heart. Can we face this together?"

Her hand found mine instinctively, and I felt a tether of strength I hadn't realized I still relied on. Love, I realized, was not always about comfort it was about facing storms side by side, even when the winds threatened to tear everything apart.

I watched him grapple with the decision, the weight of responsibility etched into his features. I wanted to shield him, to absorb the worry and pain for him, but I knew that wasn't how love worked. It required presence, yes but also courage, and the willingness to face hardship together.

"We'll handle it," I whispered, squeezing his hand firmly. "Whatever comes, we face it. Together. We choose each other, even when everything else is uncertain."

I could see the tension ease slightly in his eyes, the gratitude unspoken but palpable. The crisis wasn't gone, and the path ahead would be messy and challenging but we were ready to navigate it.

The next days became a test of resilience. Long hours, difficult conversations, and moments of frustration pressed on us like relentless waves. Yet, amidst the turbulence, there were quiet gestures of support: a hand on a shoulder, a shared meal, a late-night conversation that felt more like lifelines than words.

Through it all, I realized that love was forged not only in joy but in challenge. True connection demanded courage not just to face the storm, but to choose each other again, and again, when everything seemed uncertain.

And in that choice, silent but steadfast, we discovered a deeper truth: love is not always easy, but it is always worth the risk, the effort, the fear. Together, we could endure anything.

Healing Hands

The night was quiet, the kind of quiet that invites reflection, confession, and touch. After the chaos of recent days, I found myself drawn to her, to the warmth that had always been my refuge.

I reached for her hand first, a simple gesture, and felt the tension of the past week begin to ease. It was in the softness of her fingers against mine that I remembered: love could heal in silence, in touch, in presence without words.

"I'm here," I whispered, my voice breaking slightly, not from weakness, but from the release of holding back so long. She turned to me, eyes glistening, and I saw the mirrored relief and longing.

We leaned into each other, letting the quiet room bear witness as we rebuilt the spaces between us spaces once filled with doubt, now filling with care, understanding, and devotion.

I felt him before I saw him, the gentle weight of his hand brushing against mine, anchoring me after days of uncertainty. There was no rush, no expectation only the deliberate, slow reconnection that said more than words ever could.

I let myself lean into him, resting my head against his chest, listening to the rhythm of his heartbeat. It was steady, grounding, and in that rhythm, I found the courage to release the tension I had carried so long.

His touch traveled slowly, purposefully, across my shoulders, my back, my hands a silent apology, a promise, a reassurance. Healing, I realized, wasn't just in grand gestures or declarations; it was in the quiet intimacy, the attentiveness, the patient presence of someone who truly sees you.

We lingered in that quiet intimacy, hands entwined, breaths aligning. The world outside could wait; this moment was ours alone. Pain, fear, and uncertainty had not disappeared, but they were tempered by the presence of one another, softened by understanding and trust.

It was a revelation: love could mend wounds not only in words but in gestures, in shared silence, in the deliberate choice to hold and be held. And as the night deepened around us, I felt it hope, restored and tender, filling the spaces where doubt once lingered.

For the first time in a long time, we didn't just survive we healed. Together.

Growth in Silence
The days following the healing were quieter, yet they carried a weightier kind of beauty. I found myself noticing the small shifts how we moved through the world with a gentler patience, how our silences were no longer empty but filled with understanding.

I reflected on the mistakes I had made, the moments I had allowed fear to dictate my actions. And in that reflection, I felt growth not the loud, celebratory kind, but the subtle, steadfast evolution of someone learning to love with intention.

Each choice became deliberate: a compliment without expectation, a presence without demand, a listening ear that honored her voice. I realized that growth wasn't just about ambition or achievement it was about becoming someone worthy of trust, patience, and shared love.

I, too, felt the quiet transformation within myself. The past months had tested me, carved new depths into my resilience, and taught me the value of patience not only with him, but with myself.

I saw the strength in surrendering control, the courage in speaking truth even when it trembled on my lips, the beauty in letting love evolve without forcing perfection. Each day, I discovered facets of myself I had ignored or feared: the capacity to forgive, to listen, to hold steady even when uncertainty loomed.

And as I watched him grow alongside me, I understood a deeper truth: love was not static. It demanded attention, nurturing, and the willingness to embrace both joy and hardship with equal reverence.

We sat together in the quiet evenings, sharing our reflections without needing to speak, our presence saying what words could not. Growth, we realized, was not measured by grand gestures but by the evolution of hearts willing to stay, learn, and adapt.

The past no longer loomed like a shadow, but served as a mirror showing us who we were, who we could become, and how our shared journey could continue with grace and intention.

And in that stillness, I felt it: love had grown not in noise or display, but in the patient, silent commitment to seeing each other fully and choosing one another every day.

Full Circle
The city lights flickered like stars fallen to earth, painting the evening with gold and amber hues. I walked beside her, feeling the rhythm of her steps match mine, each heartbeat a quiet confirmation of the journey we had traveled together.

We had faced storms, navigated distance, confronted doubts, and unveiled truths long hidden. And now, in this moment, it all felt like a thread drawing us inexorably toward each other. The past the mistakes, the pain, the silence was no longer a weight. It was the foundation upon which we stood, stronger and more aware of the fragility and brilliance of love.

I reached for her hand, holding it firmly, deliberately, as though to seal every promise unspoken. "We've come full circle," I murmured, voice low, resonant with everything we had endured. "And yet... it feels like a beginning."

I squeezed his hand, feeling the warmth and steadiness that had become my anchor. I thought of every quiet conversation, every touch, every shared glance that had carried us through darkness into light. The past had tested us, but it had also shaped us shaped us into something resilient, tender, and enduring.

"Yes," I said softly, letting the words linger between us. "Full circle, but also forward. We carry what we've learned, and we carry each other. Always."

The air around us vibrated with unspoken understanding. We didn't need declarations or grand gestures. The truth of our bond was in the simple act of standing together, hearts aligned, hands clasped, souls entwined.

The night embraced us, and for the first time in a long while, silence felt like celebration. Love was no longer a storm to survive, but a current to navigate with grace and awareness.

We walked slowly, letting the city fade around us, letting the stars above witness our quiet triumph. It was not perfection we celebrated it was choice, commitment, presence, and the courage to keep showing up for one another.

And as we paused at the bridge overlooking the river, the reflection of lights dancing on the water mirrored our journey: turbulent, luminous, and endlessly moving forward.

We smiled, fingers still entwined, and in that shared glance, we understood: love in silence had carried us here and now, together, we were ready for everything yet to come.

*To the hearts that survive storms,
To the souls that choose each other again and again,
To love that grows in silence,
And blooms quietly in presence, trust, and courage

This is for you.

May the echoes of yesterday guide,
May the hands you hold steady the way,
And may love, in all its quiet brilliance,
Carry you full circle... and beyond.*

Chapter 7–*Self-Improvement, Love, and Shared Ambitions*

Morning Light
The morning arrived like a soft exhale, spilling gold across the edges of the room. I watched her sleep for a moment, the quiet rise and fall of her chest reminding me of the fragility and resilience that lived within her. It was in these still moments, untouched by words or obligations, that love felt most profound simple, steady, and undeniable.

I traced the curve of her hand as it rested on the bed, marveling at how even the smallest details seemed monumental now. The past, with its shadows and storms, had given way to a fragile clarity: that presence mattered more than perfection, that every choice we made could be an offering to the life we were building together.

Rising slowly, I brewed coffee, the aroma filling the room like a quiet promise. This was our life now not perfect, not without fear, but rich in its intimacy, in its small, deliberate joys. And in that warmth, I felt the pulse of possibility, of journeys yet to be taken, side by side.

I woke to the gentle hum of the city and the soft scent of coffee curling through the room. The sunlight caught his silhouette, painting him in quiet brilliance. I felt the weight of yesterday's storms lift slightly, replaced by a tentative hope that perhaps the world could be kinder now, or at least more patient with us.

He moved around the room with deliberate care, aware of me without saying a word. That awareness, that consideration, spoke louder than declarations ever could. It reminded me that love lived in attention, in the shared breath of mornings and evenings, in the silent affirmations of presence and choice.

Stretching, I reached for his hand, finding it already extended, fingers warm and certain. "Good morning," I whispered, and he smiled, the corners of his eyes crinkling in recognition of all we had endured.

We sipped our coffee slowly, letting the world beyond the window wait. There were no plans, no urgent matters, only the shared heartbeat of a couple rediscovering the quiet power of everyday life.

In that morning light, I understood: love was not just surviving storms or overcoming doubt it was finding sacredness in the ordinary, and courage in the simple act of being present, together.

And as the city stirred around us, we felt it hope, unspoken but palpable, anchoring us to each other and to the possibilities of everything yet to come.

Unspoken Dreams
I watched her from across the room, fingers tracing the edges of a notebook I hadn't seen before. Her brow furrowed slightly in concentration, and I realized she was sketching plans dreams I hadn't been invited into yet. Not because she excluded me, but

because some parts of our hearts are private, even to those we love most.

It struck me then: love wasn't just about being together in moments of calm it was about witnessing the silent ambitions, the quiet fears, and still choosing to stand by each other. I wanted to reach across and ask her about the dreams she hadn't spoken aloud, but I paused. Some things needed time, and trust was a delicate rhythm, not a demand.

I sipped my coffee and let her be, feeling pride swell quietly. She was unafraid to grow, to imagine, to push herself into spaces that challenged and inspired her. And in that quiet courage, I found a renewed admiration and love that ran deeper than words could capture.

I felt his gaze before I saw it, a familiar weight that both comforted and unnerved me. I had kept these plans close, unspoken, because I feared disrupting the fragile balance we had worked so hard to rebuild. Yet, his presence reminded me that ambition and love need not compete they could coexist, intertwined yet independent, like two melodies in harmony.

"I didn't mean to keep secrets," I said softly, not looking up. "It's just... some things feel too fragile to speak until I'm sure."

He moved closer, brushing a finger along the edge of the notebook. "I understand," he said gently. "I don't need all the answers right now. I just need to see you daring to dream. That's enough."

Relief and warmth washed through me. His words were a quiet permission, an acknowledgment that our love was strong enough to hold both shared moments and individual aspirations.

The room hummed with possibility, the air heavy with unspoken promises and gentle understanding. Dreams were no longer threats they were bridges, linking our individual growth to the life we were building together.

In that quiet coexistence, I realized: love was not just about presence or compromise it was about embracing the unknown in each other, witnessing growth, and finding joy in both shared victories and private triumphs.

And as the sunlight spilled across the floor, warming our joined hands, I felt it: a future unfolding, fragile yet full of hope, each unspoken dream a step toward it together.

Distance Between Us

The train station was a blur of motion faces rushing, wheels clattering, announcements fading into white noise. Yet all I could focus on was her. She stood there, suitcase at her side, eyes tracing mine with quiet hesitation.

Distance had never been our enemy, yet now it felt different. Work obligations, travel, and responsibilities pulled us into separate orbits. And while I trusted her implicitly, I couldn't ignore the subtle ache in my chest a reminder that love, even strong love, felt fragile when stretched across miles.

"I'll call when I can," I whispered, trying to embed reassurance in my tone. "Every day, even if it's just a word."

Her hand lingered in mine, reluctant to let go. "I'll wait," she said softly, eyes steady, yet betraying the shadow of worry that mirrored my own.

We parted then, our fingers finally releasing, and I felt the weight of absence settle immediately. The station bustled on, indifferent to our quiet struggle, yet every step I took forward was tethered to the thought of her waiting somewhere, miles away.

I watched him disappear into the crowd, each step pulling him further from me, and my chest ached in ways silence could not contain. I understood the demands of life and career, but that didn't ease the tension between longing and fear.

I clutched my own bag tighter, replaying his words, the warmth of his hand, the look in his eyes. Even in distance, love demanded presence not just in calls and messages, but in faith, patience, and the quiet act of holding onto what mattered most.

"I'll be patient," I whispered to myself, grounding in the knowledge that absence could be a test, but also an opportunity to grow, to reflect, to strengthen the threads that bound us.

The days apart stretched longer than either of us anticipated. Calls were brief, messages hurried, and the physical absence a constant reminder of how intertwined our lives had become. Yet even in the separation, we found ways to stay present: a text that arrived just when the day felt too heavy, a voice note that made distance shrink, a memory revisited to remind us that we were still together.

Distance was not defeat it was a challenge, a mirror reflecting both vulnerability and resilience. And in that quiet tension, we discovered a deeper understanding: love could endure absence, but it required trust, patience, and the courage to remain tethered even when the world demanded distance.

Temptations and Doubts

The city was alive with opportunity and noise, and with it came attention he hadn't expected. Compliments, invitations, subtle admiration from strangers it was flattering, yes, but it carried a weight I couldn't ignore. Every look, every word, reminded me of how fragile trust could be, even in the strongest bonds.

I found myself thinking of her constantly, questioning the right balance between professional allure and personal loyalty. Could I navigate admiration without letting it erode the foundation we had rebuilt? The thought tightened my chest a reminder that love demanded vigilance, not just passion.

In the quiet of my hotel room that night, I reached for my phone, rereading her last message, her words a tether to reality: *We trust each other. We choose each other.* And in that simple phrase, I found both guidance and reassurance.

I noticed subtle changes in him before he spoke longer pauses on calls, distracted glances, a slight hesitation in tone. My mind, usually calm and reflective, began to spin with questions, small doubts that threatened to creep into my heart.

It wasn't just the physical distance; it was the awareness of the world around him, the attentions he might receive, the uncertainties that distance magnified. I knew that love required trust, but I also knew that trust wasn't blind it was active, conscious, and fiercely protective of the bond we shared.

I sent a short message, simple but deliberate: *I trust you. But I need us to stay present, even when we're apart.* Her words were less a demand than a reminder a promise to ourselves, a shield against the subtle temptations that life inevitably brought.

The days that followed were an exercise in patience and conscious choice. Each interaction, each decision, became a reflection of the bond we were committed to protecting. Small moments of reassurance calls in the morning, messages in the evening were lifelines that bridged the physical and emotional distance.

Temptations and doubts would always exist, whispers at the edges of even the strongest love. But what mattered was the courage to face them openly, to reaffirm commitment, and to choose each other consistently, even when the world tested the limits of trust.

And in that careful, deliberate navigation, we discovered a new strength: love not just endured, but deepened, proving that fidelity of heart could outlast even the most persistent uncertainties.

Letters Unsent

It arrived unexpectedly a bundle of letters, tied neatly with a ribbon, each one folded with care and addressed in handwriting I recognized but hadn't seen in years. My pulse quickened as I read the first line, the weight of unsent words pressing on me as if they carried the power to change everything.

These letters were from her, written in moments of doubt, longing, and vulnerability sentiments she had never shared, moments she had kept tucked away, waiting for a time she felt safe enough to reveal them.

I felt a mix of awe and guilt. Awe at her courage to articulate what she felt, and guilt for the times I hadn't been present enough to hear these truths when they mattered most. Holding them, I realized that love often lives in the words we never speak and the courage it takes to finally let them see the light.

I had almost forgotten those letters, tucked away during nights when distance and doubt weighed too heavily. They were written in moments of uncertainty, a testament to the fragility of hope and the courage it takes to love fully, even when unseen.

When I saw him holding them, eyes tracing the lines I had written, I felt exposed but understood. These letters weren't confessions they were bridges, reaching across time and space, hoping he would understand the depth of my heart, even when words had failed me in person.

"I never meant for them to change anything," I whispered, voice barely audible. "I just... wanted you to know me, even in the moments I felt lost."

He looked up, eyes soft, comprehension and reverence mirrored there. "You've always been brave," he said. "These words... they make me love you even more."

We sat with the letters between us, reading, reflecting, and connecting across the delicate vulnerability they represented. Each unsent word became a testament to trust, patience, and the silent endurance of love.

The past, once weighted with uncertainty, now felt like a foundation a reminder that honesty, even delayed, could strengthen the bond between two hearts willing to receive and honor each other's truths.

And in the quiet aftermath, I understood: love is not only about the words spoken, but also about the courage to reveal them when the time is right, and the wisdom to accept them without judgment, only with understanding and presence.

Confronting Shadows
The quiet of the evening carried a weight I hadn't anticipated. Shadows of the past lingered not outside, but within me echoes of mistakes, insecurities, and moments I feared had left scars on her heart.

I wanted to reassure her, to offer words of love and certainty, but I realized that some shadows demanded more than words they demanded acknowledgment, understanding, and action.

"I'm afraid," I admitted softly, the confession feeling strange and heavy. "Afraid that I might not always protect what matters most... afraid that distance and doubt could undo us."

She didn't flinch. She simply reached for my hand, grounding me with the warmth and certainty of presence. "We all have shadows," she said. "But they only define us if we let them. Let's face them together."

I had felt it too the subtle tremor in our bond, the lingering uncertainty that distance and unspoken fears had planted. But now, seeing him willing to confront his own doubts, I felt a courage stir within me.

"I've been afraid too," I confessed, voice soft but unwavering. "Afraid that I wouldn't be enough, that my past could hurt what we're building... afraid that love alone isn't always enough."

He tightened his grip on my hand, and in that gesture, I felt all the reassurance I needed. Shadows existed, yes but together, we could illuminate them with honesty, empathy, and shared strength.

We sat in the dim light, letting our confessions linger without judgment. The air was heavy with vulnerability, yet it carried a strange relief the weight of silence lifted by the courage to speak.

In that quiet confrontation with our fears, I realized that love was not the absence of darkness it was the presence of light, steady and unwavering, in spite of it.

And as the night deepened around us, we understood: shadows could exist, doubts could linger, but our commitment to see, to hear, and to hold each other was stronger than any fear that dared to enter our hearts.

Silent Retreat

The cabin was isolated, surrounded by tall pines and the quiet hum of the forest. No emails, no calls, no obligations only space. I had chosen this retreat not to escape her, but to escape the noise of life so I could return to her with clarity, patience, and renewed presence.

I walked along the edge of a still lake, sunlight shimmering across its surface, and let my thoughts wander. Past mistakes, unspoken fears, the subtle cracks in our trust they all came into focus. But in the stillness, they seemed less threatening. Reflected in the water, they were part of a larger, enduring landscape, not isolated storms.

I realized that love, like this lake, could be still yet deep capable of holding both turbulence and serenity without losing its essence.

I had chosen my own space that week a small apartment by the sea, where waves crashed and retreated, rhythmically echoing the cadence of my thoughts. I wrote, reflected, and allowed myself to sit with emotions I often tucked away in favor of smiles and reassurance.

The distance between us was not absence; it was a conscious pause. A way to understand ourselves better, so that when we reunited, the love between us would be unburdened by doubt and filled with intention.

I traced letters in my journal, words I hadn't dared speak aloud, and realized that solitude didn't isolate me from him it sharpened my awareness of the bond we shared, deepening appreciation for what we had and what we could nurture together.

Though miles apart, our hearts remained tethered. Calls were brief and deliberate, messages thoughtful, each exchange a thread connecting us across space. The retreat was not about separation it was about preparation: to face the world together with steadiness, to return to each other fully present, fully aware, and fully committed.

And in that intentional silence, we discovered something profound: love is strengthened not only by togetherness, but by the courage to step back, reflect, and grow individually and as one.

The forests and the waves bore witness to our quiet evolution, and in the echo of nature's rhythms, we both understood: distance, when chosen with purpose, could deepen intimacy in ways proximity never could.

Reunion and Reckoning
The airport was alive with motion, but my eyes sought only her. I spotted her across the terminal, standing with quiet grace, a suitcase at her side and a soft smile that made everything else fade. Time apart had sharpened my awareness of her presence how

indispensable she had become to the rhythm of my life.

As I approached, our eyes met, and the world seemed to pause. Words felt unnecessary; the years, the distance, the fears we'd confronted all condensed into the simple act of reaching for her hand.

"I've missed you," I whispered, though it barely scratched the surface of all I felt. "Every day, every hour, I've realized how much you mean to me."

Her smile widened, eyes glistening, and I knew that the pause had not weakened us it had strengthened us, preparing us for a reunion not just of bodies, but of hearts, fully present and fully aware.

I felt his approach before I saw him, the familiar pull of recognition that made my heart flutter and steady at the same time. When he reached me, the world melted into quiet no noise, no crowd, only the gravity of our shared bond.

"I've missed you too," I admitted, voice trembling with relief and love. "Being apart made me realize how much we carry in silence, and how much we need to share in presence."

We held each other then, long and unhurried, letting the months of distance, reflection, and growth settle into warmth and understanding. This was more than reunion it was reckoning. A reckoning with fears faced alone, lessons learned in solitude, and the conscious decision to return to each other stronger, more resilient, and more intentional.

The airport, once chaotic, became a sanctuary for our connection. Each gesture, each touch, carried meaning beyond the visible. We laughed softly, shared small confessions, and listened with patience to the echoes of growth that had emerged in our time apart.

Reunion was not the conclusion of struggle— it was the acknowledgment that love thrives in both absence and presence, that vulnerability and courage are inseparable, and that the commitment to face challenges together is a choice renewed every day.

And as we left the terminal hand in hand, stepping into the evening light, we felt it the unspoken promise that no distance, no fear, no shadow could sever the bond we had consciously, courageously chosen to nurture.

Foundations of Forever

The home we had returned to after our separate retreats felt different warmer, yet charged with a sense of purpose. I watched her arrange flowers on the table, sunlight catching the edges of her hair, and felt a quiet certainty settle in my chest.

This was more than comfort; it was foundation. Every challenge we had faced, every distance endured, every fear confronted, had built a base stronger than any walls or furniture could offer. Our love had matured into something deliberate, intentional a structure meant to endure.

I took her hand, feeling the pulse of life and trust between us. "We've come far," I murmured. "Not just in distance or time, but in understanding. I want us to keep building, to plan... not just for today, but for everything ahead."

Her eyes softened, reflecting gratitude and hope. "I want that too," she whispered. "A future built on trust, respect, and shared dreams. A forever we create together, brick by brick."

I felt the weight of his gaze, steady and reassuring, as I considered our life ahead. Planning, discussing, dreaming it was no longer abstract or distant. We had survived trials and distance, navigated doubts and shadows, and now we were ready to intentionally craft a life together.

We spoke of careers, family, personal ambitions, and shared responsibilities not as constraints, but as pillars upon which our love could stand. Every decision was deliberate, every conversation a layer of care and foresight.

"I trust us," I said softly. "Not because life will be easy, but because I know we'll face everything together, with courage and honesty."

His smile mirrored mine, and I realized that foundation wasn't just about structures or plans it was about presence, commitment, and the continuous choice to nurture what we held most dearly.

We sat together, hands intertwined, letting the sun's glow anchor us in the moment. Love, we understood, was no longer merely a feeling; it was a conscious act, a deliberate construction of trust, respect, and shared vision.

Foundations of forever are built quietly, in choices made daily, in patience, in listening, and in the courage to face the unknown together. And in that stillness, we felt it: a life ahead that was ours to shape, fortified by everything we had endured, and illuminated by the unwavering certainty of our bond.

Embracing Change

The days that followed felt like a gentle tide, shifting and reshaping the landscape of our lives. New opportunities appeared career advancements, collaborations, and unforeseen responsibilities but now, we faced them together, grounded in the knowledge that our bond could withstand transformation.

I watched her adapt to each challenge with quiet grace, marveling at her resilience. Change, once daunting and intimidating, now felt like a companion, a rhythm we could move with rather than against.

"We've learned to bend without breaking," I said one evening, holding her close. "To let life reshape us, but never let it reshape us apart."

Her head rested against my chest, warmth radiating, and I felt the truth of that statement resonate: love was not a static force. It grew, evolved, and demanded flexibility yet its roots, nurtured by trust and intention, remained steadfast.

I felt the pulse of life accelerating around us, each shift demanding adaptation and attention. And yet, I no longer feared change. With him by my side, I found courage not only to face it, but to embrace it.

Every adjustment became a shared venture a test of patience, communication, and trust. Together, we navigated schedules, priorities, and ambitions, learning to listen, compromise, and celebrate victories, no matter how small.

"Change doesn't have to be frightening," I whispered. "It can be a reminder of how far we've come, and how far we can go, together."

He smiled, eyes reflecting pride and admiration. Indeed, love had transformed into something dynamic, alive, capable of holding both growth and stability, challenges and joy, dreams and reality.

We walked through the evolving landscape of our lives hand in hand, aware that every shift, every twist, every new horizon was part of the journey we had consciously chosen. Change was no longer a threat it was a canvas on which we could paint our shared story, deliberate, intentional, and beautiful.

And in the quiet glow of evening, I understood: embracing change was not surrender, nor was it loss. It was affirmation of love, of partnership, and of the courage to grow together, always moving forward while holding fast to the foundation we had built.

Shared Horizons

The car wound along the cliffside road, the ocean stretching endlessly to the horizon, waves catching the last blush of sunlight. I glanced at her, seated beside me, a quiet smile playing across her lips, eyes reflecting both curiosity and wonder.

This journey was more than sightseeing; it was a symbolic step forward. Every mile, every curve in the road, mirrored the path we had traveled together the highs, the lows, the uncertainty, and the discovery. And yet, here we were, moving forward not apart, but in tandem, hearts aligned like the rhythmic pulse of the sea.

I reached for her hand, squeezing it lightly. "Horizons," I murmured. "Not just places we go… but the life we choose to build together. Always moving forward, always side by side."

Her fingers intertwined with mine, and I felt the quiet reassurance that, no matter what lay ahead, we would meet it together anchored in trust, patience, and shared vision.

I leaned slightly against him, letting the wind tug gently at my hair and the sound of waves fill the spaces between us. Every glance at the horizon reminded me of the expansiveness of life and of love.

This journey was more than physical. It was a reaffirmation of commitment, of growth, and of the intentional choice to face the unknown together. I felt the weight of the past dissolve, replaced by the steady thrill of possibility.

"I love that we can dream together," I said softly. "Horizons aren't just places they're choices, goals, memories we create along the way."

He nodded, eyes reflective. "And we'll continue to find them, as long as we keep walking side by side."

The sun dipped lower, painting the ocean in streaks of amber and rose. We paused at a viewpoint, silent, absorbing the vastness of the world and the intimacy of our shared journey.

Horizons were no longer intimidating they were invitations. Invitations to grow, to explore, to deepen understanding, and to continue choosing each other, every day, through both certainty and uncertainty.

In that quiet embrace, I realized: love is not only a destination, but a journey full of shared horizons, endless possibility, and the courage to navigate them together.

Love in Silence

The room was quiet, yet it vibrated with presence her presence, the echo of shared laughter, the warmth of hands intertwined. I watched her, bathed in the soft glow of evening light, and realized that love's most profound moments often existed not in grand gestures, but in the quiet, unspoken acts of devotion.

I reflected on the journey we had taken: the distance endured, the doubts faced, the shadows confronted, and the horizons embraced. Each challenge, each silent test, had brought us closer to the essence of what we had chosen: each other, unconditionally, intentionally, and with reverent patience.

"Love isn't always loud," I whispered to her, voice low but steady. "Sometimes it exists in silence, and in that silence, it speaks the loudest."

I felt the weight and warmth of his words, a gentle affirmation that resonated in the spaces between us. Love in silence was not emptiness it was presence, attentiveness, and unwavering commitment.

I traced a finger along the back of his hand, marveling at how we had grown, not just together, but within ourselves. Every pause, every reflection, every quiet choice to understand rather than react had strengthened the bond we had vowed to protect.

"Yes," I breathed softly. "Silence can carry everything words sometimes fail to convey. And in that, we have found our forever."

We sat together, hands intertwined, hearts synchronized, letting the quiet envelop us. The world outside could wait; the city's chaos, the responsibilities, the uncertainties all diminished in the presence of shared understanding.

Love in silence was more than endurance; it was intentionality, patience, and the courage to remain fully present. It was a language written in glances, gestures, and steadfast trust a language only we understood completely.

As the night deepened, we closed our eyes together, the rhythm of our breathing, the warmth of our hands, and the unspoken promises between us forming a sanctuary.

And in that silence, I knew: love had found its most profound expression not in grand declarations, but in the quiet, unwavering choice to be present, to hold, and to journey forward, side by side, into every horizon yet to come.

*To the hearts that endure quietly,
To the souls that choose presence over words,
To love that blooms in patience and trust,
This is for you.

May your silences speak volumes,
May your touch anchor storms,
And may your love, steadfast and intentional,
Carry you forward together, always.*

Chapter 8–*Growth, Challenges, and Relationship Deepening*

Dawn of Change

The first light of morning spilled across the city, brushing the edges of buildings with a tentative warmth. I stood by the window, coffee in hand, and let the quiet wash over me. Life had shifted in subtle, undeniable ways since we had embraced our shared horizons. Opportunities and responsibilities pressed against the edges of our carefully built world, reminding me that love, while strong, must coexist with growth and change.

I watched her from across the room, absorbed in her journal, pen gliding across the page with steady, deliberate strokes. Each word, each pause, seemed to map her inner landscape her dreams, her reflections, her quiet anxieties. I marveled at her courage: the way she balanced presence with ambition, intimacy with independence.

Change was approaching, like the first ripple across a calm lake. And while I welcomed it, I also felt the weight of the unknown. But in her gaze, when she finally looked up and met mine, I found reassurance. Whatever came, we would face it together, grounded in trust, in love, and in the unspoken promises that had carried us this far.

The morning air carried a subtle chill, brushing against the windowpanes and stirring the curtains. I wrote in silence, letting thoughts flow onto paper before they could settle into the corners of my mind. Change was imminent I could feel it in the shifts of our lives, in the new responsibilities, in the quiet pull toward unknown horizons.

I looked up as he stood by the window, strong yet contemplative, and felt that familiar blend of comfort and awe. He understood, even without words, the delicate balance of growth and love, of ambition and presence.

"Morning," I whispered, voice soft. He turned, smile slow and certain, and in that small exchange, I felt the unspoken acknowledgment: whatever changes lay ahead, we would navigate them side by side.

The city stirred outside, oblivious to the quiet revolution within our shared world. Life was shifting opportunities, challenges, and new possibilities pressed against the edges of what we had built. But we embraced it with patience, presence, and intention, knowing that love is most resilient when it evolves alongside the lives it sustains.

And in that dawn of change, we discovered something profound: growth need not threaten love, and the unknown need not breed fear. As long as we chose each other every day, in silence, in words, and in presence everything else could unfold with grace.

Silent Conversations
Even in shared spaces, silence had its own language. I noticed the way she furrowed her brow as she worked through a new project, the slight hesitation in her responses during our morning call, the pauses that lingered just a moment too long.

I didn't want to pressure her, nor did I wish to impose my assumptions. Instead, I learned to listen differently to the weight of her silences, to the subtle rhythm of her breathing, to the unspoken currents beneath every glance.

Sometimes, silence could speak louder than words. And in those quiet moments, I felt the depth of our connection, the trust we had cultivated, and the resilience it demanded to navigate changes together without losing presence.

I felt him there, even in the quiet spaces between our conversations. The distance created by responsibilities and new ambitions was real, yet in silence, I sensed his awareness his patience, his attentiveness, his unwavering commitment.

Some thoughts were too delicate to voice immediately: doubts, fears, small insecurities that whispered beneath the surface. But even in withholding words, I knew he understood me. The depth of our connection allowed us to communicate without interruption, to feel each other's presence even when speech was unnecessary.

"Silence isn't absence," I thought, tracing a finger along the edge of my notebook. "It's attention. Presence. A language of its own."

That evening, we sat across from each other, work spread between us, conversation sparing but meaningful. The quiet held no tension only awareness, patience, and shared understanding.

Silent conversations had become our way of navigating change. They reminded us that love wasn't always about words; it was about noticing, acknowledging, and honoring each other's inner world. And in that quiet communion, we discovered a profound truth: even when life shifted, even when challenges emerged, our bond remained steadfast, fluent in the unspoken language of care and presence.

External Pressures

The office hummed with urgency, deadlines pressing in from all sides. Yet no matter how chaotic the world outside our home became, my thoughts were tethered to her the steady pulse of her presence in my life.

Work, expectations, and societal demands threatened to pull focus, yet I realized that the challenge was not external it was the way I allowed these pressures to affect us. In every decision, every meeting, every obligation, I had to consciously choose balance, ensuring that the demands of life did not erode the sanctuary we had built together.

I paused, breathing deeply, and sent her a simple message: *Thinking of you. See you tonight.* Small, deliberate. A reminder that amidst noise and expectation, our bond remained unwavering.

Family expectations, professional milestones, and unrelenting social obligations pressed around me like a tightening tide. It was easy to feel pulled in multiple directions, to forget that our love required nurturing beyond the logistics of life.

I sensed his presence even when apart, the way he adapted, adjusted, and reached across the miles with words, gestures, and thoughtfulness. In the silence between texts and calls, I felt his steadiness a reminder that partnership meant weathering external storms together, not letting them determine the course of our hearts.

I paused from my work, closing my laptop, and whispered softly to myself: *We can navigate this. Together.*

That evening, when we reunited, the world outside seemed to fade. Conversations about work, expectations, and obligations were deliberate but gentle. Each shared glance, each touch, reaffirmed that external pressures could not dilute the bond we had consciously chosen to protect.

Love, we realized, was not only about quiet mornings or stolen moments it was about resilience, adaptability, and mutual awareness. The pressures around us were inevitable, but our response to them anchored in respect, patience, and presence defined the strength of our union.

And in that quiet evening, we understood: life's external demands would never outweigh the intentional care, silent understanding, and unwavering commitment we offered each other every day.

Secrets and Shadows
The envelope sat on the kitchen counter, innocuous at first glance, yet heavy with unspoken significance. Its contents were not a threat, but a reminder: the past has a way of lingering, even when love is steadfast.

I opened it carefully. Letters, old photographs, fragments of memories things she had kept private, perhaps unsure of when or if she should share. I felt a surge of tenderness and curiosity, but also the fragile weight of responsibility: how do we honor the past without letting it shadow the present?

I folded the letters gently, placing them back on the counter. My mind traced her journey, the resilience that had carried her through moments I could never fully know. I realized that love demanded not only acceptance, but reverence for the stories that shaped her both spoken and silent.

I watched him examine the envelope, careful, thoughtful, as if handling something sacred. Vulnerability was never easy, yet here it was, laid bare in small pieces of paper and memory.

My heartbeat quickened not from fear, but from trust. The shadows of my past were not a threat to us; they were reminders of the person I had become and the love we now nurtured together.

"I didn't know when to give these to you," I whispered softly. "I wasn't sure if they belonged in the light yet."

He looked up, eyes gentle, unwavering. "Everything that is part of you belongs with me," he said. "The past doesn't weaken love it shapes it, teaches it, and makes it stronger."

We sat together, the envelope between us, letting the weight of history settle without fear. Shadows were no longer something to hide from they were truths to honor, threads in the tapestry of our shared existence.

Love, we realized, was as much about understanding the past as it was about building the future. And in that acknowledgment, we discovered that vulnerability could be a bridge, not a barrier a quiet testament to trust, patience, and the courage to embrace each other fully.

In the gentle glow of evening, with letters, memories, and shadows acknowledged, we reaffirmed what had always been true: love is not diminished by honesty; it is strengthened by it, carried forward in silence, trust, and unwavering presence.

Unspoken Choices

The evening air was thick with unspoken thoughts. I watched her across the living room, her expression contemplative, as if weighing decisions that neither of us had yet dared to voice.

Life demanded choices career opportunities that pulled in opposite directions, responsibilities that demanded attention, and dreams that sometimes seemed incompatible. Yet the most delicate challenge was navigating these without fracturing the love we had so carefully cultivated.

I approached quietly, settling beside her. "Whatever decisions come, we'll face them together," I said softly. "Even if they're hard, even if they're complicated we choose each other first."

Her eyes met mine, reflecting both relief and trust. The unspoken tension softened, replaced by the knowledge that love is not absence of difficulty, but a commitment to navigate it together.

I had wrestled silently with the crossroads before me. Every choice carried weight not only for me, but for us. There were opportunities that promised growth, yet they demanded sacrifices and compromises.

I sensed his presence, patient and unwavering, and felt a quiet courage rise within me. Love was not about always knowing the right answer, but about leaning into the partnership we had built, trusting that together we could balance ambition, responsibility, and heart.

"I don't want to make the wrong choice for us," I admitted softly. "But I know that with you beside me, we'll find the way."

He smiled gently, squeezing my hand. "There is no wrong choice when we choose each other," he replied.

We sat together in quiet contemplation, letting the weight of decisions rest between us without panic or haste. Love, we realized, thrived not in certainty, but in shared resolve.

Unspoken choices were not burdens they were opportunities to reaffirm trust, to listen deeply, and to embrace the complexity of life together. In silence, we found clarity; in presence, we found courage.

And as the evening deepened into night, we understood that love is most resilient when decisions, even unspoken, are navigated hand in hand, hearts aligned, and intentions clear.

Moments Apart

The apartment felt emptier than usual, the quiet amplifying the absence of her presence. For the first time in months, our paths diverged for a few days she had commitments across the city, and I had responsibilities I could not postpone.

Yet in the solitude, I discovered the subtle beauty of reflection. I thought about the choices we had made, the trust we had nurtured, and the patience that had carried us through challenges before. Distance, even brief, became a mirror, revealing the depth of my reliance on her presence and the expansiveness of my love.

I walked through our shared spaces slowly, tracing the edges of memories: the coffee cup she had left on the counter, the jacket draped over the chair, the soft hum of the city through the window. Each item was a quiet reminder of connection, proof that even in separation, we remained tethered.

The train hummed beneath me, city lights blurring past the window as I leaned back, letting thoughts drift. Being apart from him was not loneliness it was a space to examine my own heart, to assess fears, ambitions, and the quiet truths I sometimes buried in the busyness of our lives.

I wrote in my journal, reflections that I would later share, revelations that had emerged only because of distance. I realized that love was not possession or constant proximity, but trust, presence in thought, and intention carried across miles and minutes.

"I miss him," I admitted silently, "but I also understand him better in absence."

Our brief moments apart became lessons in patience, trust, and self-awareness. Texts were concise but meaningful; calls were thoughtful but restrained, leaving room for reflection rather than obligation.

Distance revealed that love could grow even when bodies were separated, that presence was not only physical but emotional and intentional. We learned to honor individual needs while maintaining the bond that tethered us, understanding that moments apart could strengthen, rather than weaken, our shared journey.

And when we reunited, the embrace was deeper, infused with appreciation for both the togetherness and the space that allowed love to mature in quiet resilience.

Realizations

Reunion brought a clarity that the separation had quietly nurtured. Watching her settle back into our shared space, I felt a renewed awareness of the depth of her influence on my life.

Moments apart had revealed patterns I had overlooked the subtle ways I held back, the unspoken expectations I carried, the need to be present not only in action but in intention. I realized that love was not simply a feeling but a continuous choice, an ongoing cultivation of patience, empathy, and attentiveness.

"I see now," I thought, watching her laugh softly at something mundane, "how essential it is to nurture both her world and mine without losing sight of what binds us."

I had returned with a lighter heart, the quiet reflection during our time apart having unveiled truths I hadn't acknowledged before. I saw the depth of our reliance on each other not in neediness, but in the comfort of trust, the security of understanding, and the courage to show vulnerability.

I noticed small things about him,his attentiveness, the way he anticipated my thoughts, the patience in his gestures that I had sometimes taken for granted. Realizations bloomed quietly: love was not only about grand declarations, but also the subtle consistency of care, the unwavering presence through life's fluctuations.

"I understand him more," I whispered internally, "and in understanding, I choose him more fully."

That evening, we sat together in the living room, the air between us calm yet charged with understanding. Words were sparse, yet every glance, every touch, communicated volumes. Realizations were shared without speech: the appreciation of growth, the acknowledgment of effort, the recognition of mutual reliance and respect.

We understood that love is strengthened not by absence alone, nor by proximity alone, but by the conscious awareness of both by the patience to see, the courage to learn, and the humility to grow together.

And in that quiet intimacy, we discovered a profound truth: the most enduring bonds are forged not only through shared experiences but through the insights gained when hearts and minds are open to reflection, individually and as one.

Reconciliation

Tension lingered between us not in anger, but in unspoken friction. A small disagreement over priorities had surfaced, subtle but persistent, like a shadow at the edge of our shared light. I realized that reconciliation wasn't about assigning blame; it was about understanding, listening, and realigning hearts.

I approached her gently, careful not to crowd the space she needed. "I know we're both tired," I said softly. "And I don't want this to grow into something bigger than it needs to be. Can we just... talk?"

Her gaze met mine, guarded yet open. In that instant, I understood that reconciliation was not a single act, but a process one that required patience, empathy, and humility.

I had felt the tension too, small yet undeniable, a ripple that disrupted the calm we had nurtured. I wanted to resist defensiveness, to approach the situation with clarity, but emotions had a way of tightening around the heart.

When he spoke, the softness in his voice and the care in his eyes reminded me of why we had chosen each other. "We can talk," I replied, letting my guard soften. "And we will honestly, patiently, and without judgment."

I realized that reconciliation was not about winning or conceding; it was about returning to the shared foundation of trust, love, and respect, even when disagreements arose.

We sat across from each other, speaking carefully, listening intently. Words were deliberate, pauses meaningful, and empathy abundant. The disagreement, once a source of tension, became an opportunity to strengthen communication, deepen understanding, and reaffirm the trust that anchored our relationship.

By the end of the evening, we held each other quietly, the friction dissolved, replaced by renewed connection. Reconciliation had not erased the challenge, but it had transformed it into insight, growth, and a reaffirmed commitment to navigate life's uncertainties together.

In that quiet embrace, we understood: love is not a perfect journey, but a deliberate choice, continuously renewed through listening, presence, and the courage to reconcile differences with care and patience.

Foundations of Renewal

The sun rose gently over the city skyline, painting the buildings with gold, and I felt a renewed sense of purpose. After the reconciliation, our connection had shifted subtly but profoundly closer, stronger, more intentional.

I watched her prepare breakfast, the familiar rhythm of her movements grounding me in gratitude. I realized that love, like life, required constant tending. Foundations were not built once; they were reinforced daily, in gestures, words, and choices both large and small.

"Let's create a life that reflects us," I said softly, drawing her attention. "Not just surviving day-to-day, but intentionally building, planning, and nurturing our shared dreams."

Her smile, bright and knowing, answered before words could. I understood then that renewal wasn't just a moment it was a commitment, a conscious choice to strengthen the pillars of our relationship continually.

I felt the weight and warmth of his words, a reminder that love is active, not passive. Renewal demanded attention, reflection, and courage the courage to revisit goals, dreams, and priorities with intention.

I reached for his hand, feeling the solidity of his presence. "We've grown through challenges," I said softly. "Now it's time to build on what we've learned to make our love more resilient, more aligned with our true selves."

Every plan we discussed, every goal we set, every quiet promise we made together became part of a renewed foundation stronger because it was deliberate, informed by reflection, and anchored in mutual respect.

We spent the day mapping out dreams, both practical and emotional. Careers, travel, family, personal growth all became shared projects, anchored in trust and intention. Our home, our routines, and our hearts were spaces of conscious creation, reflections of the bond we had fought to protect and deepen.

Renewal was not a single act but an ongoing process one that required listening, presence, patience, and deliberate care. And in that process, we discovered that love could evolve without losing essence, growing richer and stronger in ways only intentional commitment could achieve.

As evening fell, we sat together, hands intertwined, feeling the quiet certainty that the foundation we were building was not only enduring but vibrant, capable of sustaining both challenges and joy.

Embracing Life's Flow

Life, I realized, was rarely linear. Opportunities, setbacks, and unexpected twists arrived without invitation, demanding flexibility and calm. But with her by my side, change felt less like turbulence and more like rhythm a current to navigate together.

I watched her move through her day with effortless focus, adapting to challenges while remaining present in our shared life. In her, I saw the embodiment of resilience: the capacity to bend without breaking, to flow without losing direction, to embrace uncertainty with courage.

"Flow isn't passive," I murmured quietly, almost to myself. "It's a deliberate dance with life moving together, attuned to each other, even when currents pull differently."

I felt the currents of life tug at us, subtle and sudden, yet I no longer feared them. Together, we had built a foundation capable of weathering unpredictability strong, flexible, and rooted in trust.

I paused to reflect on how far we had come: the lessons learned in silence, the growth discovered in separation, the love reinforced through challenge. Life's flow was no longer daunting; it was an invitation to move consciously, to navigate each twist and turn hand in hand.

"I can trust the journey," I whispered internally. "Because we're navigating it together."

Evening came, soft and golden, and we sat on the balcony, watching the city breathe below us. Conversations were light but intentional; laughter mingled with thoughtful pauses. Each decision, each shared glance, each gesture was part of a larger rhythm our rhythm.

Embracing life's flow was not about controlling every outcome but about cultivating presence, patience, and adaptability. Love, we realized, was a river sometimes swift, sometimes gentle but always navigable together, as long as we remained attuned to each other and the current of life.

In that quiet evening, we discovered a profound truth: harmony does not exist in perfection, but in the conscious choice to move forward together, adjusting to life's rhythm, and holding steady in the face of change.

Shared Dreams

We stood before the blank canvas of possibility, each of us holding visions that had once existed only in private corners of our hearts. Now, they could merge, coalesce into a life designed deliberately, consciously, and lovingly.

I listened as she shared aspirations small and grand alike each one a window into her soul. I realized that shared dreams were more than compromise; they were collaboration, a way to honor individuality while creating unity.

"Let's build this together," I said, taking her hand. "Not just hopes, but plans. Not just wishes, but reality."

Her eyes shone with trust, determination, and joy. And in that moment, I understood that dreams shared were no longer fragile they became living structures, strengthened by intention and presence.

I felt a thrill in articulating dreams that had once been solitary. Career aspirations, travel plans, creative projects, and even the quiet dream of a peaceful home all became intertwined with his vision, forming a shared constellation of possibility.

The excitement was not only in achieving them but in knowing we would pursue them together, supporting, encouraging, and celebrating each milestone. Dreams, I realized, were amplified when two hearts worked in tandem, guided by mutual respect and unwavering commitment.

"We can make anything real," I whispered, leaning into him. "As long as we keep moving together."

Evening light filtered through the windows, casting long shadows across our plans spread on the table. Maps, sketches, lists, and notes each a thread in the fabric of our shared future.

Shared dreams were more than ambition they were trust, patience, and courage incarnate. We discovered that vision became reality not just through effort, but through alignment, understanding, and the steadfast choice to pursue life hand in hand.

And as night fell, we held each other quietly, feeling the weight and beauty of possibilities yet to unfold. Love was no longer just present it was forward-looking, intentional, and alive in the shared dreamscape we had chosen to cultivate together.

Love in Continuum

The night sky stretched endlessly above us, stars scattered like fragments of memory and hope. I held her hand, feeling the steady rhythm of her pulse, a quiet affirmation that what we had built was alive, enduring, and ever-evolving.

Love, I realized, was not a static state but a continuum a journey of presence, patience, and intention. Each challenge, each quiet conversation, each moment apart and together had added depth and texture, creating a bond resilient enough to endure uncertainty yet flexible enough to embrace growth.

"We've come far," I whispered, voice low. "And yet, this is only the beginning."

I leaned into him, the warmth of his presence a reminder of the constancy we had chosen amidst life's shifting currents. Reflection brought gratitude: for lessons learned, for moments of silence that spoke volumes, for dreams shared and nurtured.

Love, I understood, was ongoing a deliberate weaving of trust, vulnerability, and understanding. It was a continuum that demanded attention, courage, and devotion, yet rewarded us with depth, intimacy, and an unwavering sense of unity.

"I see it too," I replied softly. "A love that grows, shifts, and endures... endlessly."

We sat beneath the stars, the city quiet below, enveloped in the soft embrace of night. Words became unnecessary; our connection existed in glance, touch, and shared breath.

Continuum was not merely about duration but about evolution honoring the past, embracing the present, and envisioning the future with intention and care.

In that stillness, we recognized a profound truth: love is not measured by the absence of challenges, but by the strength to navigate them together. It is not only a feeling, but a choice a deliberate, enduring commitment to presence, growth, and unity.

And in the quiet night, with stars as witnesses, we understood that our journey would continue ever unfolding, ever deepening, ever ours.

*To those who choose each day anew,
To hearts that bend yet never break,
To love that endures the currents of life,
This is for you.*

*May your silences be full of understanding,
Your touch carry reassurance,
And your love remain an endless continuum
Growing, evolving, and steadfast, always.*

Chapter 9-*Anchored Hearts and Dreams Realized*

The First Light

The horizon glimmered with the first hint of dawn, a quiet promise spilling across the sky. I stood at the balcony, coffee warm in my hands, and let the city awaken below. Life had shifted again new responsibilities, new opportunities, new possibilities but through it all, the steady anchor of her presence remained.

I watched her move through the kitchen, calm yet purposeful, a rhythm that mirrored the quiet resilience I had come to admire. Change was inevitable, but with her, it no longer felt intimidating; it felt navigable.

"Every day is a beginning," I thought, "and today is ours to embrace, together."

The soft glow of morning illuminated the room, painting familiar corners with a sense of possibility. I inhaled deeply, savoring the quiet before the rush of commitments and decisions. Life was opening new doors, each one requiring courage, patience, and trust.

I glanced at him on the balcony, silhouetted against the rising sun, and felt a surge of gratitude. Change was less daunting because he was there not just beside me, but attuned to my pace, my dreams, and my fears.

"I can face anything," I whispered softly, "because we face it together."

We shared the early moments without words, letting the quiet morning speak volumes. The world outside could wait; for now, it was just us, attuned to each other, grounded in presence, and ready to embrace the first light of a new chapter.

In the stillness, we understood a profound truth: beginnings are never solitary, and the dawn of change is brightest when shared with someone who sees, honors, and walks with you.

Whispered Dreams

The night had settled softly, wrapping the city in a quiet hush. I watched her from across the room, pen in hand, as she scribbled into her journal with deliberate care. Each word seemed to capture not just thoughts, but fragments of her soul ambitions, hopes, and dreams she sometimes whispered only to herself.

I felt the familiar pull to lean closer, to ask, to probe but I restrained myself. Love, I reminded myself, often spoke in listening rather than questioning, in presence rather than interruption. Her dreams were sacred; my role was to witness, to support, and to walk beside her as she made them real.

In the hush of the evening, I whispered internally, *May her dreams unfold, and may I be worthy of walking that path with her.*

I paused mid-sentence, sensing his gaze without turning. His presence was steady, unobtrusive, like a lighthouse guiding me through both calm and storm. Writing in silence allowed me to articulate desires that words spoken aloud sometimes failed to carry fully ambitions too fragile to voice, fears too delicate to expose.

I reflected on the future, on possibilities that shimmered like distant stars. With him, I felt brave enough to hope, bold enough to plan, and secure enough to embrace the uncertainty of pursuing those dreams.

"Every dream becomes clearer when shared in trust," I whispered, even as my thoughts remained unspoken.

The room hummed with quiet energy the energy of hope, intention, and mutual understanding. Our whispered dreams did not require immediate action or declaration; they thrived in the space between us, nurtured by presence, attention, and shared care.

We discovered that love was not only in grand gestures or words of affirmation, but in the respect for each other's inner worlds the dreams, fears, and aspirations that often remained unspoken, yet deeply understood.

And as night deepened, we sat together in that shared silence, feeling the invisible threads of ambition and hope weave us closer, preparing us for the challenges and opportunities the future would bring.

Shifting Tides

The rhythm of life had changed. Projects at work demanded more time, opportunities arrived with sudden intensity, and the currents of responsibility seemed to pull in multiple directions at once. Yet amidst the tide, my thoughts were never far from her,her presence a steady anchor in the midst of constant motion.

I noticed her subtle signs of strain: a frown that lingered just a beat too long, a sigh when emails stacked on her desk, the way her hand trembled slightly as she poured coffee. I understood that love meant recognizing these shifts before they became storms, responding not with impatience, but with care.

"Change is inevitable," I whispered to myself, "but together, we can navigate it."

I felt the pull of responsibilities stretching me thin, like a sail caught in sudden wind. Family expectations, career challenges, and life's unpredictable demands tugged at my focus. Yet even in the swirl, I felt him near—through messages, glances, and the quiet knowledge that he observed without judgment and understood without explanation.

I reminded myself that resilience was built not in isolation, but in partnership. "We may be tested," I thought, "but we do not face it alone."

Even as tides shifted, I sensed a rhythm forming a balance between pressure and presence, ambition and love.

That evening, we reunited in our shared space, exhausted yet connected. Words were few but intentional; gestures spoke volumes. The day's pressures became opportunities for support, the swirling tides a reminder that life demanded adaptation and collaboration.

Love, we realized, was not only about navigating calm waters but about embracing shifts, anticipating currents, and adjusting sails together. In that quiet evening, we discovered that challenges were not obstacles but invitations to listen more deeply, to care more intentionally, and to grow more resiliently together.

And in the gentle closing of the day, we understood that when hearts remain aligned, even the shifting tides cannot erode the bond we have nurtured with patience, trust, and unwavering presence.

Hidden Currents

Even in calm moments, I sensed subtle undercurrents beneath her smiles and steady composure. A hesitation here, a quiet withdrawal there tiny ripples of thought she hadn't voiced. I realized that love demanded more than presence; it demanded attention, empathy, and the courage to address what remained unspoken.

I approached gently. "Is there something on your mind?" I asked softly, careful not to press, careful to leave room for honesty.

She met my eyes, fleeting doubt crossing her features. "I... I don't know if I should say it," she murmured.

In that pause, I understood: hidden currents were not threats, but signals opportunities to listen deeply, to create space for vulnerability, and to strengthen the foundation of trust that anchored us.

I felt him there, perceptive as always, noticing the parts of me I often kept hidden even from myself. Fears, insecurities, and lingering uncertainties floated beneath the surface currents I had learned to navigate silently, out of habit, out of caution.

Yet his presence invited courage. "I can share," I whispered internally, "because he will understand without judgment."

Speaking aloud was not easy, but it was transformative. In naming the hidden currents, I felt their weight lighten, replaced by a renewed sense of clarity, trust, and alignment.

That evening, we sat across from each other, allowing words to flow slowly and carefully, honoring both what was spoken and what remained unspoken. Hidden currents became bridges, revealing fears, dreams, and desires that had waited patiently for acknowledgment.

Love, we realized, thrived not only in open skies but in the delicate navigation of shadows. Emotional clarity was born from patience, honesty, and the willingness to explore the depths together.

And as night wrapped around us, we discovered that even beneath hidden currents, connection could grow stronger rooted in trust, empathy, and the quiet courage to meet each other fully.

Decisions in the Dark
The night was heavy, not with silence, but with the weight of choices unspoken. Career shifts, relocation possibilities, and personal ambitions tugged at both of us, each demanding consideration and courage. I felt the tension of responsibility and the pull of love, knowing that every decision had the power to shape not only our lives but the bond we had cultivated.

I studied her quietly, seeing the same contemplation mirrored in her eyes. "We can face the unknown together," I said softly, "even if we cannot see the outcome yet."

The darkness of uncertainty was less intimidating with her beside me. Decisions, I realized, were not obstacles but opportunities to strengthen trust, to communicate openly, and to choose each other first, even amidst complexity.

I felt the weight of possibility pressing against the edges of my mind, heavy yet not unbearable. Each path presented promise and risk, and the responsibility of choice felt magnified in the quiet intimacy of our shared life.

His presence was steady, a constant reminder that we were not navigating this alone. "We don't need perfect answers tonight," I whispered inwardly. "We only need honesty, patience, and alignment."

In that moment, I realized that courage was not the absence of fear, but the willingness to confront uncertainty together hand in hand, heart with heart.

We spoke in measured tones, each word deliberate, each pause intentional. Options were weighed not with urgency but with reflection; emotions were expressed without blame. The darkness became a canvas for connection, a space where trust and empathy illuminated the paths ahead.

Decisions in the dark revealed the strength of our bond. Even when outcomes were uncertain, our alignment, patience, and shared commitment acted as a guiding light. Love, we understood, thrived not in certainty, but in the conscious choice to navigate life's shadows together.

By the time dawn approached, we had not resolved every question but we had reaffirmed the most important truth: no decision could overshadow the foundation of trust and love we had built.

Lessons in Absence

The apartment felt unusually quiet without her presence. A business trip had taken her across the city, leaving a void that was both physical and emotional. At first, the silence pressed against me like a weight, but soon, I realized it was a mirror reflecting how much her presence had become intertwined with the rhythm of my life.

In her absence, I discovered patience I hadn't fully recognized, the ability to observe my own thoughts and habits with clarity. I missed her laugh, the warmth of her hand, the effortless way she made our space feel alive but in the emptiness, I also saw the strength of what we had built.

Love, I realized, was not diminished by absence; it was refined, measured not by proximity, but by trust and resilience.

The train hummed beneath me, carrying me through the city and into moments of reflection. Being away from him was not loneliness it was clarity. I could examine my ambitions, my fears, and my priorities without distraction, while still feeling anchored by his presence in thought and memory.

I wrote notes to him I wouldn't send yet, small reminders of appreciation, love, and longing. I realized absence had a subtle gift: it sharpened understanding, illuminated emotions, and strengthened connection in ways that constant proximity could not.

"I can trust the bond we've built," I whispered silently. "Distance does not sever it—it deepens it."

Our brief separation became a canvas for growth. Calls were intentional but not constant; texts were thoughtful rather than habitual. The absence emphasized presence in a new way each message, each shared memory, each anticipation of reunion became an act of care.

We discovered that love flourishes not only in shared spaces, but also in moments of self-reflection, resilience, and patience. Absence was no longer a void; it was a lesson, an opportunity to strengthen our hearts and reaffirm our commitment silently, yet profoundly.

And when we finally reunited, the embrace was deeper, infused with gratitude and renewed understanding. Love, we realized, could endure both proximity and distance, growing richer with each lesson learned in absence.

Illuminated Truths

Reunion illuminated more than her smile it revealed insights about both of us. Time apart had offered clarity, exposing patterns I hadn't noticed, strengths I had taken for granted, and vulnerabilities I had avoided confronting.

I realized that love was not merely about presence, but about understanding: noticing her unspoken needs, acknowledging my own, and bridging the space between with patience and empathy. In the quiet of our shared moments, truths emerged effortlessly, like sunlight filtering through clouds.

"I see now," I reflected, "how growth is intertwined with reflection, and love deepens when truth is met openly."

I studied him as we settled into the comfort of shared silence, noticing small gestures I had overlooked before the way his hand rested lightly on mine, the quiet attentiveness in his gaze. The absence, the challenges, and the conversations of the past weeks had revealed truths I had buried beneath routine and comfort.

Love, I understood, was as much about insight as affection. Understanding the depths of each other's fears, dreams, and rhythms was the foundation upon which trust and intimacy could flourish.

"I know him better," I whispered internally. "And in knowing him, I choose him more fully."

We sat together, letting the quiet speak. Words were unnecessary; our understanding resonated in glances, touches, and the shared calm of being fully seen. Illuminated truths were not always easy, but they were liberating they cleared the fog of assumption, revealed the contours of intention, and deepened the roots of our connection.

We discovered that love thrives when both hearts commit to seeing clearly, embracing growth, and acknowledging the vulnerabilities that make connection real. Truth, we realized, was not a threat but a gift guiding us, shaping us, and fortifying the bond we shared.

As night fell, we held each other in quiet gratitude, knowing that illuminated truths had transformed challenges into opportunities, uncertainty into clarity, and love into something enduring, resilient, and beautifully alive.

Renewal of Trust

Even in strong bonds, cracks appear not from betrayal, but from misunderstanding, assumptions, or unspoken expectations. I sensed a subtle hesitation in her, a quiet test of patience and understanding. Trust, I realized, was not a static gift; it was a living entity, requiring care, renewal, and intentional effort.

I approached gently, words measured, tone soft. "I want us to be honest," I said. "Even when it's hard. Even when it's uncomfortable. I want us to rebuild every part of us if needed."

Her gaze met mine, a mixture of vulnerability and hope. In that moment, I understood: renewal was an active choice, a deliberate act of love, and an opportunity to fortify the foundation that had carried us through so much already.

I felt the weight of unspoken doubts, subtle insecurities that had crept in despite the strength of our bond. His words, gentle and intentional, opened a space where I could release them safely, knowing that my honesty would be met with patience, not judgment.

"I can trust him," I reminded myself. "And trust is strongest when it is consciously renewed."

Speaking openly, sharing fears, and acknowledging uncertainties became an act of intimacy, not weakness. I realized that trust was not merely given it was nurtured, repaired, and celebrated in the quiet resilience of mutual commitment.

We spoke slowly, carefully, listening more than we spoke. Every pause was deliberate, every acknowledgment intentional. Misunderstandings were cleared, unspoken fears addressed, and the foundation of our relationship reinforced with deliberate care.

Renewal of trust was not a dramatic event, but a quiet, profound process an ongoing choice to honor honesty, patience, and love. And in that stillness, we discovered that even the subtlest fractures could transform into opportunities for deeper connection and understanding.

By night's end, we embraced, not merely as partners, but as allies, knowing that trust had been reaffirmed and strengthened, ready to face life's next challenges together.

Anchored Hearts

The morning light felt different that day softer, more certain, as if the world had paused to recognize the calm that comes after storms of doubt. I watched her prepare for the day, noticing the subtle confidence in her movements, the quiet alignment of purpose and presence.

I realized that love, like a ship at sea, needed anchors not to restrict movement, but to provide stability amidst change. Our shared values, trust, and respect had become those anchors, grounding us even when life's currents pulled in unexpected directions.

"Anchored hearts," I thought, "are free hearts able to navigate the world with courage, clarity, and commitment."

I felt the security of being seen, understood, and supported. Challenges had come and gone, lessons had been learned, and through it all, the essence of our bond had strengthened. Anchored hearts were not stagnant; they were resilient, capable of bending without breaking, of embracing change while remaining rooted in shared values and love.

"I am grounded," I whispered internally. "And in that grounding, I can soar."

We spent the evening planning, dreaming, and reflecting, not in urgency but with deliberate care. Conversations flowed effortlessly, decisions were made thoughtfully, and moments of laughter and quiet acknowledgment interwove seamlessly.

Anchored hearts meant that even amidst the unpredictability of life, we could move forward with alignment, confidence, and harmony. Our connection was no longer just a feeling it was a living, breathing structure, resilient and enduring.

As night fell, we held each other, feeling the depth of our bond, the certainty of our alignment, and the profound strength of hearts that were both anchored and free.

Flow of Life
Life had a rhythm, I realized not always predictable, rarely still, but always moving. Challenges, opportunities, and unexpected turns flowed like a river, demanding attentiveness and adaptability. With her by

my side, the current felt less like turbulence and more like shared motion a dance in which both of us moved in synchrony with life's unpredictable tempo.

I watched her navigate her day with grace and focus, her energy flowing between personal ambition and our shared life. "Flow," I thought, "is not passivity. It is conscious movement, aligned with purpose and love."

I felt the subtle push and pull of life, a mix of excitement, pressure, and unpredictability. Yet with him, the currents no longer felt overwhelming. Together, we had learned to bend, to adjust, and to move without losing balance or sight of each other.

I realized that embracing life's flow required trust not just in each other, but in ourselves. "We are capable," I whispered internally, "capable of moving with change without losing our center."

Evening descended with quiet serenity. We walked through the city streets, hand in hand, observing the ebb and flow of life around us the soft hum of traffic, the distant laughter of strangers, the calm of shared presence.

Flow of life, we discovered, was not about controlling the current but navigating it together, with trust, awareness, and patience. Every decision, every choice, and every shared moment became part of a larger rhythm, a harmonious movement that strengthened our connection.

By nightfall, we understood a subtle truth: love, when anchored in trust and guided by conscious presence, could embrace change, flow with life, and emerge more resilient and luminous on the other side.

Dreams Realized
The morning air carried a subtle sense of triumph, not loud or boastful, but quiet and fulfilling. Months of dedication, patience, and shared effort had begun to bear fruit. Projects once only imagined were taking shape, opportunities we had carefully nurtured were unfolding, and our shared ambitions were becoming reality.

I watched her with admiration as she celebrated her own milestones, her eyes reflecting the joy of accomplishment. Dreams,

I realized, were not merely wishes they were commitments, cultivated daily through perseverance, trust, and mutual support.

"We dreamed together," I thought, "and together, we made it real."

I felt a profound satisfaction, a sense of alignment between effort and outcome. Each success, whether personal or shared, was a testament not only to hard work, but to the bond that sustained us. Our dreams had grown from quiet whispers into living achievements, strengthened by collaboration, understanding, and unwavering encouragement.

"I can see it now," I whispered internally, "our efforts manifesting, our hopes materializing, and our love growing richer through the journey."

Evening arrived with gentle serenity. We sat together, reflecting on milestones achieved and challenges overcome, letting gratitude and quiet celebration fill the space between us. Dreams realized were more than tangible outcomes they were proof of alignment, trust, and shared vision.

We discovered that love and ambition were not in conflict, but in harmony. Each success, each accomplishment, deepened our connection and reinforced the joy of shared purpose.

In that calm night, we held hands, hearts brimming with gratitude and possibility, knowing that the journey of building dreams together was ongoing and that the fulfillment of one chapter was only the beginning of the next.

Love Eternal
The night sky stretched infinitely, a tapestry of stars mirrored by the depth of my thoughts. I held her hand, feeling the familiar warmth that had become both anchor and compass. Years of shared experiences, challenges, and triumphs had transformed our love it was no longer merely passion or affection, but a living, evolving force that shaped and sustained us.

I realized that love was eternal not because it was untouched by time, but because it endured, adapted, and deepened with every choice, every challenge, and every quiet moment of connection.

"We have built something beyond words," I whispered internally. "Something eternal."

I leaned into him, feeling the weight and grace of our shared history. Our love had weathered storms, celebrated victories, and grown richer through reflection and renewal. It was resilient yet tender, steadfast yet adaptable a love that could embrace the uncertainty of life without fear.

"I see it clearly now," I thought. "Love is eternal when nurtured, honored, and lived fully moment by moment, choice by choice."

We sat beneath the stars, words unnecessary, presence sufficient. Every heartbeat, every breath, every gentle touch spoke volumes telling the story of patience, growth, trust, and unwavering commitment.

Love eternal was not about perfection, but about choosing each other continuously, embracing life's currents together, and finding beauty in both triumphs and trials. It was the culmination of shared dreams, illuminated truths, and anchored hearts a love that moved, flowed, and grew, endlessly.

And in that quiet night, with the city sleeping below and the universe above, we understood a profound truth: love, when cultivated with intention and grace, is not bound by time. It is eternal living, breathing, and ever-present in the hearts of those who choose it daily.

*To those who endure and grow,
To hearts that bend yet never break,
To love that embraces change and remains steadfast,
This is for you.*

*May your bonds be anchors in life's flow,
Your trust renewed with patience and care,
And your love eternal, evolving, and luminous
A light that guides, strengthens, and endures.*

Chapter 10-*The End of Love in Silence / Love Beyond Silence*

Dawn of Memories
The morning sun spilled across the room with a golden hush, touching corners long familiar

yet always new. I sat quietly, letting the light wash over memories that had accumulated like leaves along the path of our shared life. Each smile, each tear, each whispered promise returned vividly, reminding me of the journey we had undertaken together.

Time had shaped us softened some edges, hardened others but love remained the constant, the quiet thread that wove through every chapter of our story. I thought of the laughter, the challenges, the silent nights filled with reflection, and I realized that these moments were treasures, preserved not in photographs, but in the essence of our bond.

"Every dawn," I whispered internally, "carries the weight and beauty of what we have shared."

I gazed out the window at the waking city, seeing in its rhythm the echoes of our life together. Memories surfaced effortlessly: nights spent in quiet conversation, mornings drenched in sunlight, challenges overcome, and dreams fulfilled. Each recollection was imbued with gratitude for patience, for growth, and for the unwavering presence of the one who had become my anchor.

I felt a profound sense of clarity: love was more than a feeling; it was a journey of endurance, reflection, and shared evolution. Our story had not always been easy, but it had been ours crafted in silence, nurtured in trust, and strengthened by the quiet courage of choosing each other, again and again.

"Every memory," I whispered softly, "is a testament to the life we built together."

We sat across from each other, the room bathed in the gentle light of early morning. Words were unnecessary; presence was enough. Our hands met across the table, fingers entwined, grounding us in the here and now while honoring every step of the journey that had brought us here.

Dawn of memories was not just reflection it was recognition. Recognition of growth, love, endurance, and the legacy of moments lived fully. In that quiet intimacy, we understood that the past was not only remembered, but revered, and that each memory carried the promise of continued love, presence, and understanding.

And as the sun rose higher, we let the quiet settle around us, a soft acknowledgment of a life rich in love, lessons, and luminous moments that had become eternal.

Echoes of the Past

The quiet of the room was filled with echoes not of sound, but of memory. I traced the lines of our story in my mind: the first hesitant smiles, the moments of doubt, the victories that had felt impossible at the time. Each memory carried weight, a soft reminder of how far we had come and how deeply our hearts had intertwined.

I saw the lessons in every choice we had made the times we had faltered and the times we had risen. Life had tested us, reshaped us, and refined us into the people we had become. And through it all, one truth endured: love was both the compass and the map, guiding us through joy, pain, and growth alike.

"Every moment," I whispered, "has led me here to this understanding, this gratitude, this unwavering presence of her in my life."

I walked slowly through the corridors of memory, revisiting laughter, tears, whispered fears, and declarations of love. Each recollection shimmered with clarity, revealing patterns of growth, patience, and enduring connection. I marveled at the resilience we had cultivated, the trust we had rebuilt time and again, and the quiet strength of hearts committed to one another.

Some memories were bittersweet the challenges, the separations, the moments when silence had spoken louder than words but even they were gifts, shaping our empathy, compassion, and depth of understanding.

"Every echo," I reflected softly, "reminds me of our journey, our choices, and the love that has remained steadfast through it all."

We shared the space, letting our thoughts drift through the echoes of the past. Words were not necessary; understanding bridged every gap, honoring triumphs and acknowledging struggles. Each memory became a thread, weaving the tapestry of our shared existence complex, beautiful, and enduring.

In the quiet, we realized that love is not only experienced in the present but strengthened by reflection, enriched by acknowledgment, and eternalized by memory. The echoes of the past were not just reminders they were affirmations of everything we had survived, celebrated, and created together.

And as the day progressed, we carried those echoes into the present, aware that every lesson, every joy, and every heartache had prepared us to face the future with courage, unity, and an unshakable bond.

Winds of Change
The world had shifted once again. Career demands intensified, responsibilities multiplied, and unexpected challenges arose like gusts of wind against a steady sail. Change, inevitable and relentless, tested both patience and perspective. Yet I felt a quiet confidence anchored not in control, but in the trust and partnership we had cultivated over years of shared experience.

I watched her navigate the sudden currents with grace, noting how even in uncertainty, she remained grounded, present, and resilient. Life would test us, I realized, but it could not undo what we had built.

"Winds may blow," I thought, "but together, we adjust, bend, and remain steadfast."

I felt the shifts around us, subtle and sudden, bringing both excitement and unease. Life had a rhythm that could not be predicted, and yet, in his presence, the storms felt less daunting. I had learned that fear diminished when shared, that challenges were easier to face when hearts aligned, and that love was strongest when it embraced change rather than resisting it.

"We can face this," I whispered internally. "Not because the winds are calm, but because we are steady together."

Evening came with reflection. We spoke in measured tones, planned with careful deliberation, and supported each other without judgment. The winds of change were not adversaries they were catalysts, revealing the depth of our resilience and the strength of our bond.

We discovered that love, when cultivated with patience, trust, and intentional presence, could withstand any upheaval. Change no longer threatened; it became a shared challenge, an opportunity to grow closer, and a reminder that together, we could navigate life's currents with grace.

By nightfall, we embraced, hearts aligned, understanding that love was not static it was living, adapting, and enduring, capable of thriving even amidst the strongest winds.

Silent Storms

The storm did not announce itself with thunder or lightning it arrived quietly, in unspoken tensions, fleeting doubts, and the subtle weight of unresolved moments. I sensed her hesitation, the small retreats behind smiles, and the quiet anxiety that sometimes accompanied life's pressures.

I understood that love was not only about joy, but about navigating silent storms together holding space, listening deeply, and offering reassurance without rushing resolution. Patience became the anchor, and empathy the guiding light.

"Even in silence," I thought, "we can weather storms if we remain attentive, steady, and present."

I felt the tension between us, not explosive, but insistent a reminder that even enduring love encounters moments of uncertainty and fear. I longed to speak, to bridge the quiet distance, yet I feared disrupting the fragile calm that remained.

In that hesitation, I realized that trust and patience were vital. Storms were temporary; the foundation we had built over years was permanent. I drew strength from knowing that our connection could hold, even in unspoken struggle.

"Love is not absence of storms," I whispered internally. "It is the courage to face them together."

We navigated the evening with care. Words were chosen deliberately; gestures became reassurance; eyes spoke when voices faltered. The storm passed gradually, leaving clarity in its wake.

Through silent storms, we discovered that love could endure tension without fracture, that vulnerability strengthened bonds, and that the most profound growth often occurs in the quiet spaces between words.

By night's end, the calm felt earned, not granted. We held each other with awareness, gratitude, and the knowledge that even the quietest storms could deepen our understanding, patience, and unwavering commitment.

Anchored Souls

In the quiet aftermath of challenges, I felt the strength of our bond more vividly than ever. Life's trials had tested us, yet each test only revealed the depth of our resilience and the steadfastness of our connection. Anchored souls, I realized, are not defined by the absence of turbulence, but by their capacity to remain grounded amid it.

I reached for her hand, feeling the subtle warmth and familiarity that had carried me through countless storms. Our hearts, though tested, remained synchronized steady in rhythm, unwavering in trust.

"Anchoring is not restraint," I thought, "it is freedom rooted in certainty, love, and unwavering presence."

I felt the calm that comes from true grounding, the serenity of knowing that, despite life's unpredictable currents, we were aligned heart, mind, and spirit. Anchored souls do not resist change; they embrace it together, secure in the knowledge that challenges cannot sever what is intentionally nurtured.

I reflected on the journey every separation, misunderstanding, and triumph had been a thread woven into the fabric of our enduring bond. Each thread strengthened the tapestry, making our connection not only resilient but luminous.

"Anchored yet free," I whispered inwardly, "this is the essence of love that endures."

Evening settled around us, a quiet companion to our reflection. We spoke minimally, listened deeply, and held space for one another, letting presence itself communicate what words could not. Anchored souls, we discovered, are capable of facing life fully without fear, without hesitation, and with hearts attuned to the shared rhythm of love.

The night became a celebration of quiet strength, of patience, and of unwavering commitment. Our connection was no longer defined solely by passion or joy, but by the profound security of knowing that whatever winds may come, we would navigate them together, anchored in love, trust, and mutual understanding.

Shared Horizons

The horizon stretched before us like a promise, painted with the soft light of possibility. Together, we had navigated storms, celebrated triumphs, and endured challenges, and now the future felt expansive an open landscape shaped by our shared dreams and unwavering commitment.

I saw her confidence, her joy, and the spark in her eyes that had never dimmed, even after years of trials. Our ambitions intertwined seamlessly, no longer separate paths but a shared journey toward fulfillment.

"We have built this together," I thought, "a horizon where our hopes converge and our hearts remain aligned."

I gazed ahead, feeling the breadth of all we had achieved and all that awaited us. Life's possibilities were vast, but no longer intimidating, because we moved forward as one. Our shared visions personal growth, family, love, and legacy were no longer distant ideals, but tangible realities unfolding before us.

I felt gratitude and awe for the journey that had led us here, and for the partnership that made every horizon brighter.

"Together," I whispered internally, "there is no limit to what we can embrace, achieve, or become."

We walked side by side, hands intertwined, hearts synchronized with the rhythm of shared purpose. Conversations were filled with reflection, laughter, and planning, each moment reinforcing the alignment of our lives.

Shared horizons, we realized, were more than goals they were a testament to unity, trust, and love matured over time. The future, though uncertain, was no longer daunting; it was an open invitation to continue building, exploring, and living fully together.

And as the sun dipped toward the horizon, we felt a quiet certainty: that whatever came next, we would face it as we always had together, grounded in love, and inspired by the endless possibilities that lay ahead.

Illuminated Legacy
I watched the life we had built ripple outward, touching not just us, but those around us family, friends, and even strangers inspired by our shared presence. Our choices, our patience, our unwavering commitment, had created a quiet influence, a legacy shaped not by grand gestures, but by consistency, love, and authenticity.

I realized that love's impact extends beyond intimacy it illuminates paths, nurtures growth, and leaves traces of hope in hearts that observe, learn, and follow.

"Legacy," I thought, "is not what we leave behind, but what we cultivate together in the hearts of others."

I felt the resonance of our life, the echoes of love that had shaped not only our journey but the lives of those around us. Children inspired by example, friends uplifted by presence, and family strengthened by the patience, care, and empathy we practiced daily all reflected the luminous path we had walked.

I understood then that love's deepest expression is not in what is declared, but in what is lived silent, steady, and enduring.

"Our lives," I whispered internally, "are a beacon, a reflection of love cultivated, challenges met, and hearts aligned."

Evening wrapped around us, yet the light of our legacy shimmered quietly, guiding, affirming, and inspiring. We spoke little, for words were unnecessary; our presence, our history, and our alignment carried the weight of reflection and purpose.

Illuminated legacy was not about recognition, but about resonance. It was knowing that our love, patience, and intentional life together had created a ripple effect quiet, profound, and lasting.

We discovered that the true measure of love is not only in shared moments but in the enduring mark it leaves on the hearts it touches, and in the example it sets for those who witness it.

Eternal Presence
In the quiet of the evening, I felt her presence as a constant, unshakable force. Not because life had stopped moving, but because love, cultivated over decades, had become something beyond time a presence that anchored, comforted, and illuminated even the simplest moments.

I reflected on all we had endured: the storms, the triumphs, the subtle moments of growth and understanding. In each, her presence had been unwavering, steadying me, teaching me patience, and reminding me that love is not fleeting it endures, transforms, and transcends.

"Love," I thought, "is eternal when it is present in every choice, every touch, every shared glance."

I sensed him beside me not just as a partner, but as a companion whose presence had become woven into the fabric of my being. Decades of shared experiences had created a bond that was no longer measured by proximity or words, but by the quiet resonance of mutual understanding, empathy, and unwavering commitment.

I understood then that love's true power lies not in grand declarations, but in enduring presence the kind that holds steady through time, life's unpredictability, and even the inevitable impermanence of things.

"His presence," I whispered inwardly, "is eternal, and so is ours, in every memory, every heartbeat, every moment we choose each other."

We sat side by side, hands entwined, hearts aligned, aware that the passage of time could not diminish what we had built. The world around us moved, shifted, and changed, but within our connection, time held no dominion.

Eternal presence is not an absence of change; it is the capacity to remain grounded, connected, and luminous amidst life's impermanence. Love, we realized, is a living legacy steady, enduring, and profoundly transformative.

And in that quiet evening, we embraced the ultimate truth: that when love is nurtured, honored, and consciously lived, it transcends both words and years, becoming an eternal presence within the hearts it touches.

The Last Dance

The evening was gentle, like a melody played softly for two. Candlelight flickered, shadows swaying against the walls, echoing the rhythm of our shared heartbeat. I reached for her hand, and in that touch, the entirety of our journey resonated the laughter, the tears, the quiet resilience, and the unspoken devotion that had carried us through decades.

This dance was not choreographed for the world; it was ours alone a culmination of every step we had taken together, every choice we had made, every storm we had weathered. Each movement was an echo of patience, understanding, and enduring love.

"In this dance," I thought, "we are infinite, timeless, unbroken."

I felt the music, soft and deliberate, wrap around us like an embrace. Every step, every sway, every glance mirrored the depth of our connection. The years had added grace, understanding, and depth to our love, transforming it into something steady yet exhilarating, quiet yet alive.

I realized then that the last dance was not an ending, but a celebration—a recognition of the journey, the growth, and the timeless bond that had defined our lives.

"This moment," I whispered internally, "holds every memory, every joy, every challenge, and every triumph we have shared."

We moved in harmony, bodies attuned to the rhythm of life itself, hearts synchronized in quiet reverence. Words were unnecessary; every gesture, every touch, every glance spoke volumes.

The last dance was more than movement it was reflection, gratitude, and affirmation of love that had endured all trials, embraced change, and grown stronger with each passing day.

And as the final notes lingered in the air, we held each other close, understanding the profound truth: love, when fully lived, does not end. It dances on, eternal, luminous, and infinitely present within the hearts of those who nurture it.

Love Beyond Silence

The night was still, yet alive with memory and meaning. I looked at her, the one who had journeyed through every chapter of my life, and I saw more than love I saw legacy, resilience, and the quiet power of a bond cultivated with patience, trust, and unwavering devotion.

Love beyond silence is not found in grand declarations or fleeting gestures; it exists in presence, in the echoes of shared laughter and tears, in the unwavering alignment of hearts that have grown together, endured together, and chosen each other endlessly.

"In her," I thought, "I see eternity love unbound by words, unshaken by time, luminous in its depth."

I felt the culmination of years, the reflection of a life lived in tandem, in perfect imperfection. Love had carried us through storms, celebrated our triumphs, and deepened with each quiet choice, each act of patience, and every shared silence.

I realized that love beyond silence is a presence a living, breathing testament to endurance, growth, and grace. It exists in the ordinary and extraordinary, in the fleeting and the eternal, in every moment consciously chosen together.

"Our love," I whispered internally, "is not bound by endings it is eternal, luminous, and infinite."

We held each other, letting the quiet speak volumes. Every heartbeat, every shared breath, every gentle touch was a testament to the journey, the lessons, and the depth of connection we had nurtured.

Love beyond silence is the ultimate truth: that life, time, and circumstance cannot diminish what is intentional, present, and deeply rooted. It transcends speech, outlasts years, and lives on in memory, action, and the resonance of two souls intertwined.

And as the world continued its motion outside our sanctuary, we understood a profound and eternal truth: love, when fully lived, does not conclude it endures, transforms, and shines beyond the confines of silence, leaving a legacy of heart, presence, and grace.

*To the lovers who endure beyond words,
To the hearts that choose again and again,
To the souls anchored, yet free
This is for you.*

*Love beyond silence is not an ending,
But a beginning without boundary,
A light that carries forward,
A heartbeat echoing through eternity.*

www.ingramcontent.com/pod-product-compliance
Lightning Source LLC
Chambersburg PA
CBHW070916260626
47162CB00007B/2692